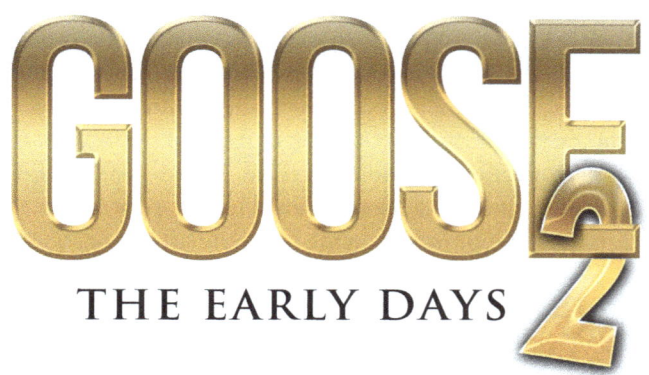

GOOSE 2

THE EARLY DAYS

FREDERICK W. PENNEY

Quantity sales special discounts are available on quantity purchases by corporations, associations, and others. For details, contact the publisher at carol@markvictorhansenlibrary.com

Orders by U.S. trade bookstores and wholesalers.
Email: carol@markvictorhansenlibrary.com

Creative contribution by Jennifer Plaza
Cover Design - DBree, StoneBear Design
Illustrations - Matt Phillips
Book Layout - DBree, StoneBear Design

Manufactured and printed in the United States of America distributed globally by markvictorhansenlibrary.com

New York | Los Angeles | London | Sydney

ISBN: 979-8-88581-095-1 Hardback
ISBN: 979-8-88581-096-8 Paperback
ISBN: 979-8-88581-097-5 eBook
Library of Congress Control Number: 2023909953

DISCLAIMER

Unless otherwise indicated, all the names, characters, businesses, places, events and incidents in this book are either the product of the author's imagination or used in a fictitious manner. Any resemblance to actual persons, living or dead, or actual events is purely coincidental. Do not try to recreate any scenes or events in this book.

CONTENTS

PROLOGUE

The funny thing about life is that relationships, circumstances, and choices determine the outcome. Or maybe I should say the journey is the outcome because life is finite. You can be happy with your life and still want to find more ways to improve. To seek contentment. Childhood friends, neighbors, departed family members, and schooldays ended decades in the past, still come to mind when asked, "How did you get here?" Of course, that question is loaded. In a matter of six or seven decades, a person goes through thousands of journeys. Waking up to a new day is a journey. Obstacles or happenstances wait, longing for resolution and acceptance. So how does one learn to embrace those hiccups that emerge? How does one overcome, endure, and maintain the necessary motivation to get back up?

Influential people would be one way to answer that question, but another would be to embrace experience. Experience is knowledge and with that, the answers emerge. A grandmother or father, a mother or brother, it does not matter. Grandfathers, sisters, aunts, uncles, neighbors; they are all a part of a person's history. There are lessons to hold from their unique wisdom. My father was an amazing influencer who knew how to work hard, teach hard, and to show love in a very unique way. He was always a parent and disciplinary first and friend second. His lessons taught each of his boys how to face all of life's challenges, which turn into learning curves. He was a man to whom I attribute my work ethic and toughness.

My grandmother was another person who gave me the wisdom to persevere and overcome. She questioned failure and turned it into a lesson. There is no such thing as failing if you keep trying. Failing is merely an experience. Search for solutions, keep getting back in the game or off the ground. This woman taught me that you could be anything you wanted if you had the motivation to get it. Did I mention she ran her own grocery store in the 1940s? She knew what she was talking about because she lived it.

Then there was my mother who taught me to keep kindness and love for all. She was a woman who taught me moral values and choices. To this day, I have not had a drink of alcohol. Not because she told me I shouldn't, but because I made up my mind not to, and I followed through.

I am the result of all those people and more. And just like William Collins, the successful attorney and entrepreneur in Goose, young Willie is a comedic force who must learn for himself; see and experience what challenges he must overcome. Will he ever admit defeat? Back down from a raging cow or bloated corpse?

To learn the making of the man, the great and honorable William Collins, I invite you to join him on his early life-changing journey while he slings plums and devours peaches in *Goose 2: The Making of a Legend.*

1
GOODBYE

"Yay!" Willie bellowed, his head hanging out of his father's green 1969 Dodge Coronet station wagon, the kind with the rear-facing back seat. His brothers bounced as the dust rolled over the back window, earning squeals of delight from the four boys.

Eddie leaned across their youngest brother, Stewart, hollering to get Willie and their other brother Mark's attention. "A train!" Eddie pointed to a distant train bridge spanning the valley. The boys pulled invisible whistle cords and hooted, imitating the train's hoots and clacks. Once called the steam trumpet, a train's series of tones in the bellows made a chord that achieved a universal communication system. Mark and Willie fought for a turn at the window.

"I wanna see," Mark whined.

"You'll get your chance." Willie, being three years older, was bigger and stronger. He won. "Wooh, wooh!" he hollered, leading his other brothers to join the locomotive commotion. Willie sat back for Stewart so he could see the caboose disappeared out of sight. "There had to be forty cars."

Eddie nodded in agreement. "They're not that long back home."

William Sr. shook his head, laughing. "Well, Cara, I think they're excited. How about you?" Willie was the spitting image of his father. When William Sr. was a young freckled boy back in Sacramento, he was a lover of all things new, especially if they were big and loud.

Cara, Willie's mother, was the complete opposite. She was a God-fearing lady from Los Angeles. The kind that kept up her hair and nails while maintaining a tidy home. Her tears started before they left their house in favor of an unknown abode in the country. More tears were shed as William Sr. drove past single-wide trailers and rundown farmhouses with grayed wood and chickens running through the yard. Gravel roads turned into dry dirt paths that kicked up dust which filled the cabin of the car. Her eyes reddened from crying and the country atmosphere.

The fair-skinned woman grimaced, her hands twisting the strap of a shiny, large pink purse. "Definitely, but ..." she raised her voice over the riled boys' banter.

William Sr. hollered over the racket, "All you boys need to mind yourselves, or you'll find yourselves in a pit of trouble."

"Aw, William," Cara said, "Don't go scaring them. Let 'em have their fun."

William Sr. frowned at her. "They need a little fear."

It didn't matter because the boys were too loud to hear their father's warning or their mother's condoning tone. Willie had Stewart's head in a lock because he elbowed him in the gut to get to the window. Mark and Eddie were rooting for each brother, an unsuccessful attempt to pry the two apart. A quick jerk of the wheel by their father ended the scuffle, bringing the attention back to the pothole filled road and rolling dirt clouds encapsulating the car. Willie smiled despite his brothers, and pictured himself standing on the top of the world in his new land, the master of his own universe, with a peach in each hand.

The move was an adventure for them all.

The Collins family was headed north of Sacramento and west of Lake Tahoe, somewhere in Northern California, to a twenty-acre parcel. It was made available when one of the large, old co-op plum farms decided to subdivide and sell off. But Willie was eleven years old and moving to the country—that's all that mattered. The awe and excitement that swelled in his belly burned raw and true. He left his childhood city home, school, and friends.

None of the things left behind mattered. Willie relished the August heat that filled the cramped space as they took turns sticking their heads out of the windows. The morning turned to noon and all they could see were peach and plum trees for miles. Hundreds of acres decorated with the small dark green leaves and golden orange and purple fruit. Willie settled against the cream leather seat. When his father pulled onto a road with a modest green farmhouse situated off the side, the boys chattered louder, scooting across the seats, taking in their new surroundings.

Two familiar faces stood in the yard, waving to the car. William Sr. barely managed to stop the car before the boys hit the ground with their feet. They threw the car doors open, Willie first, then Eddie. The two smaller boys took longer to scramble out of the seats. A large Irish setter bounced from the porch to the open car door. She barked and danced around the boys.

"Grandma, Grandpa!" Willie shouted, running up to his grandmother's open arms. His brothers followed.

Cara stepped from the car, straightened her daisy print, cornflower blue dress, and slipped on her white sunhat. "Hey, Mom and Dad."

The older man stepped up to William Sr. and shook his hand. "Good to see you, Bill. Glad to see you made it."

Willie ran back to his father's side. He watched the way his father assessed the land. The man's back was straight, his head high. The property was all plum orchards. It was a person his father knew in Sacramento who broke up the land into ten and twenty-acre parcels. Granite rocks jutted from everywhere. He remembered passing the Griffith quarry before the roads turned to dust. Willie wandered toward a rise in the field where he could see the distant mountains, purple shadows bathed in the hot California sun. The peaches and plums took a backseat to the view.

The weeds were knee-high; their Irish setter wound herself around Willie's legs. The view of the valley was massive, with 360-degree hills, railroad tracks, and a distant city. A railway bridge had upper and lower tracks that sounded like thunder when the trains rushed by. For the first time in Willie's life, he stood in a grove of trees, taking in large breaths of sweet air. The tinge of fruit fragrance mingled with the earthy undertone of beef cattle from the hundred-acre farm next door. His awe turned to joy, imprinting on his young mind what happiness should be.

"Willie," Eddie called. "Look." His older brother pointed to a tan tarp by a dilapidated barn. Willie ran to join his brother. "Come on, let's see what's under it."

Willie and Eddie each took a corner. "On three," Eddie said.

"One, two, three," they counted and pulled. Worn tools that were there from the old farm lay in a rusted pile. Shovels, metal objects that looked to be large blades, and a bunch of other wooden-handled tools hid the gem.

"You boys found a red International tractor," William Sr. declared, slapping them both on the back. "Best sort these tools and get this into the barn. If it ran once, it'll run again."

The boys were no strangers to helping and jumped in

to start the sorting. It was a way to discover what was left behind and speculate about who used them and for what. It was the most excitement Willie and his brothers ever had while working, but it was hard, and it was new. Once they sent Stewart and Mark back and forth a hundred times more than they needed, in the guise of being gentle with the fragile tools—which was Eddie's line—they were the ones left standing a fool.

"Hey, Dad," Eddie yelled. "How do we get the tractor to start?"

William Sr. came back from inspecting the old house to assess the tractor. "Well," he said and rubbed his forehead with the back of his hand, wiping away the beads of sweat threatening to run into his eyes. "It looks like the tires are flat, and it's pretty much rusted through. You know what I always say."

"There's no such thing as a problem, only a waiting solution," the boys said in unison.

William Sr. winked. "Then I guess you boys better find it. I smell Grandma's cookin' and you don't want to miss that." William Sr. left for the barn where Willie and Eddie were to take the tractor, whistling as he went.

Willie eyed an oil can with a cloth rag sticking from the top. "Hey, Eddie. What if we slick up the rusted parts? I think if we can knock some of the rust loose with a hammer, we can get the wheels to turn enough to get everyone to push her into the barn."

Eddie grabbed a wrench from the tools his younger brothers had laid out, while Willie grabbed the oil. Together, they worked on oiling and banging the wheels. They took turns beating the seized metal and saturating the parts with oil, but it was no use. The last thing Willie wanted was to admit defeat. But he was determined. "Hey, what if we tie it to something and pull it? We don't need the wheels to work."

Willie ran to the barn to tell his father. The man was repairing the ladder to the hayloft. "Dad, I think I know what to do." His father put his hammer down. The look on his face told Willie he was ready to listen. "I think the Dodge is strong enough to pull it. If we hook up the tractor, we can get it into the barn with the car."

His father looked at the barn door, then the back wall. "Did you think this through?"

The boy walked around the bay. "We can pull it up the hill, and then push it in once it's near the doors."

"Sounds like a plan." William Sr. went to get the car, and with his sons' ingenuity, the tractor was pulled to the barn.

"Why don't you boys run along before he comes up with another puzzling task," Willie's grandfather joked.

Willie took his grandfather's suggestion to heart. He motioned to Eddie, Mark, and Stewart, who were hot on his heels. Willie was a fast runner; his anticipation and excitement were pure. He hit the top of the hill among the plum trees before his brothers and waited, taking in the distant ranches.

Mark picked a deep purple plum the size of a golf ball and bit. "These are good."

Eddie grabbed a plum off the ground and flung it at his brother. The juice splatted across Mark's back. His voice cracked, making his declaration of triumph less regal, "Bullseye!"

Willie and Stewart ducked behind the orchard trees. They plucked decaying plums from the vibrant green grass and pelted Eddie. "Take that," Willie shouted. He flung plum after plum at his brother.

Mark scrambled behind a rock and gathered his own arsenal of small yellow plums from an old tree. Willie eyed him and waited for an opportune moment. When Mark popped up, Willie threw like he was pitching for the Giants. The boys dodged fruit and slid on the dry brown grass. Their laughter filled the fields until Willie saw movement behind a stone wall that separated his grandfather's parcel and the neighbor's. He didn't say a word. Instead, he clutched a ripe plum in his hand, juggled it, and aimed toward the long granite outcropping.

A boy half the size of Eddie leapt toward him, throwing a barrage of fruit at the brothers. His throwing arm was accurate and his aim precise.

"This is war!" Willie declared.

The fight was on. The foe darted and ducked, dodging every blow. Willie threw one after another. Eddie joined him. Stewart took refuge behind a protruding mound of granite while Mark kept a full inventory for his older brothers. They were all smeared with squashed plums, laughing and ducking. The lone country boy was besting the city boys.

After what seemed like hours, but Willie knew was only a matter of twenty minutes, the foe disappeared. "Where'd he go?" He turned around, scanning the trees and stone wall.

A tap on the shoulder sent a cold shiver up his spine. "Hey, good fight," an unfamiliar voice said.Willie turned slowly to assess the damage he'd caused but faced a fairly clean kid. He was half Eddie's height, but lanky. "You were only hit a few times."

"I'm faster than you," he said. "You're new, I'm Dwayne."

"I'm Willie, and these are my brothers; Eddie, Mark—who we call Stinky—and Stewart the Rat."

Cara's voice carried through the orchard to where the boys were making their introductions. "Boys, time to say goodbye."

With a sigh and hunched shoulders, the boys took advantage of the moment. Willie put out his hand to Dwayne. "You'd make a great pitcher. Glad you were around."

"Yeah, good to meet you all. Same time tomorrow?" Dwayne asked.

Eddie put his own hand out to affirm. "You, too. Tomorrow, sure."

Dwayne smiled; his mouth filled with braces. "I'll show you around. Let you meet the guys." After they shook hands, the boys went their separate ways.

When Stewart ran onto their grandparents' porch first, their grandmother stopped him at the door. "I don't know what you all were doing, but you're not tracking that in here." She pointed to the side of the house. "There's a hose and nozzle. Get cleaned up and you can have your supper." Eddie led the way, followed by Willie, Mark, and Stew.

The deep well water coming out of the hose was cold and sweet to taste. Eddie stripped to his shorts and washed the plum juice from his arms. Willie did the same but had to wash pulp and dried bits from his hair. It seemed that he was hit less but sustained more damage in the way of splattered fruit, which meant grass, pebbles, and dirt clung to him. He rinsed off his whole body and turned the hose on his younger brothers. He didn't wait for them to strip before putting his thumb over the end and spraying them down. The two boys ran around, screaming and giggling. It was Willie's perfect ending to the first amazing day in the country.

The life they left was a mere memory. Willie went to

bed exhausted yet filled with anticipation. He lay in the double bed with his three brothers, knowing they had a house to rebuild and friends in the making. Moving to the country was better than he'd hoped. A distant train crossed the bridge he saw earlier in the day, the sound lulling him to sleep. It was the first night of many where the soothing sound of creaking cars and rumbling tracks would capture his heart, showing him the music of the valley and the majesty of the rolling country hills. It was the lullaby of trains, and a sign of a day well lived.

With dreams taking hold, Willie closed his eyes and muttered, "It's okay to say *goodbye*. Sometimes, it's followed by *hello*."

Eddie mumbled, "Shut up." It was the last word spoken on that fateful day. The day that proved there was no stronger bond than brotherhood, that hard work paid off, and friends like Dwayne would be waiting, just after the rooster crowed.

2
NIGHT AND DAY

Willie moved at the start of the new school year. Prior to that, he was an elementary athlete. He was the kid that coaches chose as their runner. He was slim, quick, and had stamina fueled by an internal motivation to last through the long stretch. In academics, he was not as stellar. He didn't care for studying, though he did his homework. Willie Collins was a good kid with a passion for adventure. His United States Marine father taught all his boys to face adversity head-on and never back down from a fight. And in his new domain, he did just that.

There was still a week before the start of school. Willie awoke with wide eyes. The first morning brought a wealth of excitement. The previous night, Willie's grandfather warned him and his brother, Eddie, to rise before breakfast. "You'll be up before the rooster crows if you know what's good for you. There are hills for exploring, but not if you stick around." He winked at Willie and Eddie before taking the younger brothers to see the chicken coup. "Your Pa is sure to find work for ya."

Willie took his grandfather's words to heart. With the pheasant rooster's crow, he was up at the break of dawn and peeked through the curtains. The sun was an orange stream of light on the horizon, illuminating the plum trees on the crest of the hill. The same spot he stood to take in the Sacramento Valley views. Eddie snorted next to him, so he shook his older brother's shoulder. "Come on," he whispered. "We've got to go meet Dwayne."

Eddie rolled over. "Huh, oh, right." He rubbed his eyes. "We're meeting his guys."

The two boys scampered out of bed and grabbed their play clothes from an olive-green duffel bag they'd thrown them in before leaving their house in Sacramento. Willie had a pair of dungarees with patches sewn on the knees. They were hand-me-downs from Eddie. They both had old flannel shirts from their father and pulled them over tank tops before running down the stairs to the aroma of hot bacon grease.

"Your father's in the barn already," Grandfather said, sipping his hot tea at the table. Grandmother was at the stove frying eggs in the leftover bits of meat and grease. Willie sat and grabbed a piece of bacon before Eddie and put it on his plate. Grandmother slid a perfect, soft yoked egg onto their plates and poured orange juice into their glasses. The table was set, complete with a plate of buttered toast.

"Thank you," Willie said, glancing at the door. He

knew he'd have to help his father later with building their house, but he wanted to meet Dwayne. A new friend had a bigger appeal, which drew him away from his chair. He sat half on the seat with a foot on the floor, ready to run.

Eddie scooped up the liquid gold from the fried egg on his plate with the last bit of toast before speaking. "Thanks for breakfast, Grandma. It was great." He took his dishes to the sink and nodded at Willie.

Willie grabbed his own, put them in the sink, and finished the last of his juice. "See you later," he called as he followed his older brother out the door.

The boys decided to run behind the barn through the plum trees. Willie kept the lead until they met the neighbor's fence at the edge of an enormous cow pasture. The field was larger than any they'd seen on the drive north of Sacramento. Willie reminded his brother about their new friend's instructions, "Dwayne said to meet him by the fence at the edge of the road."

"Guess we head that way." Eddie pointed to the direction that took them uphill where the road was highest. "We drove over that crest when we got here yesterday. I thought it curved back."

"Seems like the long way around to me," Willie huffed.

Eddie shrugged. "Well, if that's where we're supposed to meet Dwayne, then let's go."

The two boys hurried, following the line of barbed wire. "I've never seen grass this high," Eddie said, pointing out the tall grass that took over the field as they neared the road. Later, they would learn it was rye grass. There were also fields of grass that served as a main source of food for the horses and cattle in the area.

Willie made it to the dirt pass before his brother. "This isn't much of a road, is it?" he joked. "No hot tar sticking to our shoes."

"Speaking of hot," Eddie said, taking his flannel shirt off and tying it around his waist. "The air's different here. Yeah, it's hot but smells."

Willie took a deep breath. The sweet aroma of plums, grass, and the distant cow pasture made his nose tingle and his cheeks flush. It brought a genuine smile to his face. The country smells imprinted on him. In his later years, he would recall that moment and relish the memory.

The country was a foreign world from what he knew. He was a transplant from Sacramento where the streets were dense with buildings, cars, trolleys, and people. Women had careers, and churches held hundreds of parishioners. Gray sidewalks lined the cobble or macadam roads. Trees were planted with purpose; the arboretum was one such location. The smell of smog, hot pavement, and people permeated the air. People varied from freshly perfumed like his mother, to that of vagrants who hadn't seen water for a year. Being the son of a woman who was a pageant-winning city girl and a father who was a city cop, Willie knew his way around the streets.

His friends were different then. He recalled the previous spring in Sacramento when his schoolmates rushed home on foot to change out of their good clothes. Willie had one thing on his mind back then, and that was getting to the ball field in time for the game. The city ball field was clean and well-kept while the country ball field was a pasture with cows in it. Weeds grew up in the field. There was no backstop other than the catcher himself, who wore shorts and a T-shirt—no mask. The kids used leftover lumber from farm projects or whatever they could find to mark the pitcher's mound and bases. The city, on the other hand, was a different world, and Willie's mind drifted back.

"Hey, Willie!" his friend Cameron called upon seeing Willie race home from school. "You comin' to the park?"

Willie glanced over his shoulder at the kid dressed in jeans with a new leather baseball glove. "Yeah, be there in a jiff." He knew he had to get his homework done before jetting out to hang with the gang before nightfall. But he was the secret weapon for his team and a guaranteed win against the rivals who dared show for an after-dinner game. It was an unorganized affair, and once the game ended or the sun dipped to the horizon, kids scattered home.

Home to Willie was a humble two-story row house

his mother Cara Collins kept neat and tidy. The windows let in the morning sun on the east when his mother opened the blinds in the living room, which he thought was huge. A set of sheer curtains hung over the blinds, shrouding the view from those within more than that of passersby—hence the need for blinds. In the back of the home was a kitchen with a small set of white, wall cabinets and a counter just large enough to hold a cutting board or dish rack. The ice box and stove were also white with chrome handles. A six-seater table sat in the small space that separated the two rooms. From there, a heavy walnut-stained staircase wound up to the second floor to the three bedrooms. The first and larger on the left was painted blue for the boys. The smaller one down the hall with the door was yellow for his parents.

Willie and his brothers shared the blue room and the contents within. They had a baseball glove, a bat, a ball, and a closet with hand-me-down clothes. Each boy had his own treasure box hidden in some facet of the room. Willie kept his under the foot of an antique iron bed that he shared with Eddie. He kept his treasure in an old metal ammo box that his father bought for him. They had gone to a military surplus store where William Sr. explained the box's use to his boys. Willie was the most intrigued, so the man made the purchase to his son's delight.

Though William Sr. didn't clarify it, Willie imagined that it might have been the actual box his father used during his time in the Korean War. He knew the man was a gunner and envisioned the box sitting on a patch of dirt in the field. The rusted gray metal had sharp edges and small hinges. It smelled old and looked even older. Willie kept important treasures in the confines: a chunk of fool's gold, a horseshoe magnet, and a Mickey Mantle baseball card his father gave him from his own childhood. It made him proud to own a piece of his father's history, but not as proud as to share his name.

Willie was named after his father in the start of a tradition. His older brother Eddie was named after his grandfather on his mother's side as an honor to the Scandinavian man. Willie always felt lucky to be second because he found the greatest honor to be named after his own father. William Sr. was not a man of many words, and his mother never broached the subject. And it wasn't like any of the boys to ask questions about parental decisions—even if it was about their own names. In the Collins house, the boys were not a part of the decision-making process. Decisions were for the adults and the children accepted whatever came their way. In fact, the adults were served their meals first, and the children second at the table. It was not in the boys' nature to question. It was exactly that way when William Sr. made the dinner announcement, "We're moving to the country."

The following Saturday morning, his mother called up

the stairs, "Boys, your father's waiting." Tears glistened in her eyes.

Willie and his brothers didn't look back before they settled in the Dodge Coronet cheering, "We're moving!" Willie yelled, an attempt to outshout his brothers. It didn't ease his mother's distress, but he was an oblivious eleven-year-old boy embarking on a new adventure.

The adventure meant leaving the state capital of California. A city founded during the California Gold Rush. With Paradise Beach on the American River and neat rows of housing, it was a mecca of sorts. People wanted the farm-to-table lifestyle. The markets had fresh local produce, and people from all ethnicities opened shops on city streets for an eclectic dining and living experience. There were no shops where they were moving, but it was well known for having a large concentration of Japanese farmers.

Eddie tossed a plum at Willie from a nearby tree and hit him in the gut.

"Hey," Willie said, clutching his stomach.

Eddie smiled, "Stop daydreamin'."

Willie blinked, "I'm not." He took a bite of the plum and stuck another in his pocket for later. As he stood wiping the juice from his chin with the cuff of his flannel, a train whistle sounded. He was no stranger to trains, but this sound was different from the ones in the city.

Back in Sacramento, the trains were fast and grounded

in history. The transcontinental railroad was completed in Sacramento, and Transurban trains provided services to those in the local city and nearby Oakland. The boys were used to those.

"Do you hear that?" Willie said. "It's like thunder."

"But it's different. Look, there are two tracks, one upper and the other lower." Eddie pointed to the tracks and rail tunnel in the distance. It was close enough that they could hear the clacking and creaking of the freight cars. The roaring sound of the eastbound train on the upper tracks was headed to Lake Tahoe. It built a fire of excitement in Willie's core as it neared. They watched as the engine pulled the cars uphill; the strain echoed in the valley less than a mile away on the top of the mountain ridge.

The lower tracks went downhill toward the south, which was the one that had put Willie and his brothers to sleep the night before. It was a noticeable difference. The sound was a rumbling moan that filled the evening quiet. A calm, soothing sound.

The boys kept watch until the train disappeared around the bend.

Willie let out a yip when the last car was out of sight. "That was awesome!" He stared at the empty tracks a moment longer. The sound had lulled his excitement to meet Dwayne. The soothing rumble had put him to sleep the night before and now it entranced him. It was the first one he heard that morning, but it wouldn't be the last.

Eddie hit him with another plum. "Come on, Dwayne's waiting."

Willie ran after his brother to the road, glancing over his shoulder for one last glimpse. It was only eight o'clock and a romp past a cow pasture, but the adventure was underway. Little did he know that the adventure would be lifelong, rooted in a passion that only the country could instill. He was a boy with an endless hunger for more, and a curiosity to fill it.

3
THE BAXTER

"**S**o, why'd we have to come all the way up here?" Eddie asked Dwayne. The boy met them on the road at the edge of Willie's grandparents' property, a gentleman's farm of two parcels for a total of twenty acres. With their parents' purchase, it gave the family thirty acres of plums, farming land enough for vegetables, and a few hens. "And why you gotta gun?"

"One word," Dwayne hissed, "Baxter."

"What's that?" Willie asked.

Dwayne waved for Willie and Eddie to follow him. The brothers stepped in line on the rutted dirt road, kicking up pebbles and dust. The older boy had on a patchwork pair of trousers and a stained white T-shirt that Willie noticed right away. He jabbed Eddie in the arm with his elbow, nodding toward their leader. Eddie cocked an eyebrow but didn't say anything.

They stayed on the road for what seemed like fifteen minutes to Willie before Dwayne ducked behind an oak tree just out of view of a small trailer that had come into view. Eddie and Willie followed. Dwayne put his finger to his lips and pointed to a spot in the grass for them to stand.

"That's Baxter's trailer, up there on the hill," he said, pointing at a silver, bullet-shaped enclosure that made Willie appreciate his tiny row house back in Sacramento.

He realized then that the houses they passed in the country were nothing like the ones back in the city. They were run down or wood with additions that seemed to be graying and falling apart. Cracked paint, crumbled concrete steps, and dirt driveways were the norm. Baxter's trailer was no exception. His barn was two times the size of Willie's home, though it had broken slats of boards with a clear smell of animal manure. To Willie, Baxter's trailer seemed a scant wider than a full-grown man laying down and the length was barely enough for a bed. "How's he live in that thing?" Willie asked.

"Hush," Eddie said. "Not everybody lives in the same kind of house. He's probably got a bathroom and one of those foldaway beds that turns into a couch."

"Well, if it was me, I'd have moved into the barn. There's enough room in there for a whole house." Willie shook his head in disapproval. "I don't know how a person can live in something so tiny."

"Shh," Dwayne hissed. "You don't want him to hear ya." He drew his gun and Willie read the name *Daisy*.

"It's a BB gun," he exclaimed.

Eddie rolled his eyes. "I know. You think people just run around with big rifles out here?"

Willie shrugged.

"Shh," Dwayne hissed again. Then he pointed to Eddie. "Baxter's as mean as it gets. He was a soldier in Vietnam. My Pa told me that when he came back, he holed up in that trailer and never comes out. If he sees you on his land, he'll take out his .22 and shoot ya." Dwayne spit on the ground as if to put an emphasis on his last statement.

Eddie shook his head. "He's just tryin' to scare us, Willie. Don't you worry, there are laws against shootin' people."

Dwayne bent down to look into Willie's eyes, "I ain't foolin'. If he sees you on his property," he drew a line across his neck and stuck out his tongue, "you'll be dead, and he'll bury you out in the field. And nobody will find you."

Willie considered what his brother told him. He was determined not to be fooled by outlandish tales from some country kid. He was from the city and people were bound to pull his leg. He stared at the windows a moment too long before he realized his brother and Dwayne had moved on, up the wood line along the road. Willie tripped over fallen branches and roots in his attempt to catch up. "Guys!" He ran as fast as his legs would carry him past the trailer at the crest of the hill and saw the two boys waiting for him on the downward stretch.

"Shh," Dwayne hissed. He waved his hand faster than Willie could see. It was a clear signal that the boy wanted Willie to be scared.

It was at that point Willie decided he wasn't playing into Dwayne's game or anyone else's for that matter. He left the wood line, stepped onto the road, and walked at a normal pace to where his friend stood. When he reached him, he folded his arms in triumph. "Well, isn't it a miracle? I lived."

"Believe me, don't believe me. You'll see." The older boy turned his back to Willie and continued down the road to a bend where a protruding granite boulder had two other boys waiting. "Patrick. Spence," Dwayne called.

The boys waved a single arm overhead. They also had BB guns, which they held barrel end down. Willie took in the patchwork pants with the front pockets sewn on the back of the tallest kid's trousers and pointed it out to Eddie.

"Psst. Eddie, look." Willie stifled a laugh. The mismatched tan corduroy pants with denim pockets caught him off guard.

"What's with the BB guns?" Eddie asked, extra loud, jogging ahead of Willie.

"Never know what or who is out here," the boy in the altered pants said. "I'm Patrick, by the way. You can call me Pat."

"And I'm Spence," the shorter blonde boy said. He was thicker than Dwayne and Pat, but not as thick as Willie and Eddie.

It was those happenstances that stuck out to Willie.

The people in his Sacramento neighborhood were not wealthy in the common neighborhoods. Willie knew his family fit in the median. They were poor, though not impoverished. But the country had a different kind of wealth. It was where Willie learned riches came in many packages. Clean air, well water, and raging cows were just the beginning. Though he found it humbling to have pants with their own pockets and clean shirts. Not that he didn't have sewn patches on his knees and reinforced belt loops, but he never had to wear a pair of pants made up of others. For that reason alone, he realized the difference in culture.

Willie stepped in line behind Eddie, bringing up the rear of the troupe. "Where we goin'?" he asked.

"Over the tracks and to the mines," Spence said. "That's why we need the guns. Too many wild beasts and . . ."

Dwayne spat in a dust-covered pile of leaves. "And murderers."

"There are no murderers here," Eddie hissed. "Stop tryin' to scare us."

Dwayne squinted at Eddie. "You ever see a dead body?"

Willie shook his head. "No."

"Be prepared, because today you just might. Ain't nobody goin' into the mines anymore. They filled with water and became a dumping ground for gangsters and the like," Spence said. He stuck his hands in his home-sewn back pockets. "You never know what you'll find if you go deep enough."

Eddie knocked Willie's shoulder with his own. "He's just goofin' on ya. Don't let it get to ya."

Willie folded his arms in front of his chest. He didn't mind jokes, but being in the middle of no-man's-land, heading to unknown territory caused his gut to clench. His father always told him to face his fears, so he swallowed it back and took the lead. "Tell me where to go because I'm leading the way. If today's the day I see a dead body, then I won't need to worry about seein' the next one."

Pat hurried next to Willie's side, "I like you; you got gumption."

The boys followed the road to a stream that separated the wood path and the lower train tracks. Rather than follow the road to the bridge on the bend, Dwayne waved for them to follow him. They watched as Spence hurdled the waist-deep water, which Eddie tried to copy. He hit the gravel on the other side, cutting his hands as he lashed out at branches to keep from sliding into the murky water. Willie was next. He also tried but fell short and ended up landing on the edge in a foot of water and mud. Pat and Dwayne laughed from the flat ground just above the shore.

"How'd you get there so fast?" Willie asked, his voice higher than usual.

Pat pointed to a board they laid across a narrow point. "You need to be more observant. Not everything has to be done the hard way."

The two brothers decided to watch the three friends. It was their grandmother's adage, 'Think before you leap.' She warned the boys to always use their heads. There were too many avenues for them to fall prey to, and it was up to them to know which would lead them down the right path. Willie thought about her warning in the literal sense and whispered to Eddie, "Thank goodness Grandma wasn't here to see that."

Eddie pursed his lips, "This stays between you and me."

Willie agreed. "Let's just hope her warning about mountain lions in the area doesn't become a reality on this trip."

Eddie sighed. "Yeah."

The late morning sun beat down on the boys. The trail Pat and Dwayne led them up proved to be a feat neither Collins boy had anticipated. The hill was a mountain. They climbed up over the protruding granite until they came to the steep hill that covered the train tunnel they saw from their farm. The three boys stepped out on the edge of the stone façade and sat, swinging their feet over the tunnel.

"Well, come on," Dwayne urged. "Ain't no train comin' to take off your legs."

"Not yet, at least," Pat said, spitting on the gravel-bedded tracks below.

Willie stepped out first. He was amazed at the width. The stone was large enough for him to scamper back if a train came or for him to lay on his stomach to feel the rumble up close. He hoped he'd get to see one. Eddie took a seat next to his brother.

"The eleven thirty is comin'," Dwayne said. "You ever sit on a train tunnel before?"

Willie shook his head. "Why would we?"

"Why not?" Spence asked.

Eddie whispered to Willie, "We'll just be smart and stay alert."

Willie didn't have to wait long. The eleven thirty train rumbled on approach. The ground shook. The boys kept their feet hanging, but Willie backed away. He rolled to his stomach and peeked over the edge. The deep groan grew louder. He covered his ears as it neared. All the boys followed Willie's lead, lying on their stomachs. As the train emerged from the tunnel, smoke hit them. The horn blew for the upcoming crossing, approximately half a mile up the track, and barreled on while the boys' hoots and hollers were swallowed by screeches and bells.

"Okay, that was cool," Eddie said.

The boys smacked Willie on the back. "That's why we sit on the tunnel." Dwayne jumped down onto the tracks. "On to the mines!"

Willie's mind raced. He was hot and thirsty. The smoke from the train took his breath away but filled him with adrenaline. He wanted more. Whatever lay ahead, he was ready. The boys ran down the hillside toward a meandering water ditch that the farmers used to water their crops. Willie raced toward it, eager to quench his thirst.

He lay flat on his stomach and reached down to the water. It was not clear. It was a little dirty, but cold. The running liquid was inviting, but he hesitated. His father always told him never to drink the water. He could get sick, but Willie's tongue stuck to his lips. His throat ached from being dry and won over his father's warning. He cupped his hands and brought the cool wetness to his lips.

"Don't drink that," Dwayne yelled. He was closing in on Willie.

Willie sipped and then took handfuls to gulp and splash on his sunbaked face and arms. "It's cool and not too dirty. I'm sure it's fine."

Eddie squatted beside him and took a handful of his own to drink. The three boys laughed. "What?"

Willie searched for Spence, Pat, and Dwayne. When he found two boys and not the third, he stood to get a better look. Upstream he saw Pat relieving himself in the river. "Eddie get away from there. They're peein' in the water."

Eddie scrambled back from the water's reach, spitting out the bit he just sipped. "Not funny, guys."

"Uh, yeah, it was," Dwayne said, slapping him on the back. "The entrance to the mine is up there. We'll cross the river in the shallows." He walked away toward the other boys. Willie and Eddie followed.

"Next time, we bring Dad's canteen," Willie said.

Eddie nodded and spit on the ground.

A ten-minute walk proved fruitful. The mouth of the mine appeared before them. The entrance was barricaded with wooden boards nailed into place, covered by long, hanging grapevines that hung from trees nearby. Pat and Spence shimmied one loose and retrieved flashlights from their pockets. The flashlights were heavy silver tubes with wide faces and required four 'D' batteries.

"We only have these old flashlights," Eddie said, hitting his to get it to work.

Willie stepped beside Dwayne. He knew going in without a light was dangerous, but he didn't want to show his fear. He had to find a way to make the adventure happen. He looked inside the opening where Spence disappeared. The space was pitch black except for the flashlight's halo. A track led to the inside depths of the mine, giving Willie an idea.

"Since we don't have good lights, let's follow the feel of the tracks today. We have to get back for chores before dinner anyway," Willie said. It was so dark that they couldn't see the tracks without some sort of light.

"Good thinking," Eddie agreed. "We should be back before dark and it's already getting on. A quick investigation will do the trick." He turned to Dwayne and the guys. "We'll have guns and better flashlights next time."

Willie made a mental note to be prepared. He didn't want to be the butt of their jokes, and he really wanted to explore the mines. He had a piece of fool's gold back in his ammo box, but his heart quickened over finding the real deal.

The boys agreed and spent a good hour following the tracks in the caverns, investigating empty dynamite boxes. Willie and Eddie handed out plums when their stomachs were audible to the others, and they used it as an excuse to get back home.

"It's gotta be near dinnertime," Willie said.

"Yeah, I think we're all hungry," Spence said, biting the fruit. "What are you guys doing tomorrow?"

"Probably working on our house, fixing fences, and putting sprinklers in the fields. Maybe the day after that we can meet up again," Eddie said.

The group of friends agreed to return while making plans for the exploration. Pat would bring sandwiches. The other boys were responsible for fruit and water. Willie was proud to have proven himself while remaining smart. Their new friends were none the wiser to his plan and continued to talk about places they wanted to show him and his brother before school started. It was the end of summer, and they were determined to stretch the adventures.

They followed the road back toward Dwayne's property. Willie was tired from climbing and wandering the mountainside. Another hill seemed like a needless and daunting task. "I still don't see how come we can't just go across the field. It's just a handful of cows."

Dwayne spit in the grass. "I told ya, Baxter will shoot you if the cows don't get you first, especially those mean mother cows."

Willie cocked his head. "You mean the bulls aren't the mean ones?"

"Ha, ha," chuckled Dwayne, "Nooo, no!"

Eddie started up the hill. "Come on, Willie. He may be pulling our leg, but at least we know this way is safe."

Willie ducked under the barbed wire that separated Dwayne's property from Baxter's. "I'll meet you on the other side. I'm not scared."

Willie strolled through the head-high grass, whistling along and swinging his arms. He glanced back at Dwayne and knew that his brother had gone the other route toward home. He was determined to prove to the country kids that he wasn't as dumb as they thought. They could only pull one over on Willie Collins so many times. After that, they were out of luck. He made it to the middle of the field before the cows noticed. A large black and white-faced cow swished her tail before wandering in his direction. He stopped whistling and stuck his hands in his pockets. When he glanced up, Baxter was at the top of the hill. Willie was in the lush green pasture. Baxter stood; his gun aimed at Willie.

4
LIFE LESSONS

Willie spotted Baxter and his gun from a distance. The first shot whizzed past Willie's head. His legs kicked into high gear. He eyed his grandparents' plum trees and ran. He ran like his life depended on it, and it did. Another shot rang out. The cow that spotted Willie took his running as a sign of aggression. She charged toward Willie, who now ducked into the long grass to keep out of Baxter's vision while also trying to increase his speed to keep the distance between him and his bovine nemesis.

The last thing Willie expected was to become fodder for both Baxter and the cow. He spotted Dwayne and Eddie at the barbed wire by the plum trees. He couldn't let Baxter win. The cow was hot on his heels when he heard Dwayne screaming, "Duck and weave, she can't move as fast!" Which was clearly not true, but an attempt to encourage Willie.

Willie knew the quickest line was a straight line, so he went to the spot he planned. He had no intention of weaving because that meant a longer stretch of time in Baxter's pasture and more opportunities to be shot. The cow increased speed and Willie felt her breath hot on his back. He eyed the fence and leapt.

Eddie held it open for him. He made it halfway through before getting his pants caught. Baxter stopped firing, but the cow was poised for action, had Willie come back through. Dwayne worked the fabric loose, but not before a fist-sized hole tore in the leg, and the barbed wire fencing sliced Willie's shin.

With blood dripping down his pants, Willie hobbled through the trees and to the house knowing Baxter missed on purpose. He was a Vietnam War veteran and only wanted to scare him. The cow was a different story. He wanted to hide the wound from his mother because she had iodine, and he wanted no part of that. He would also need to explain why his pants had blood stains and a giant hole.

Willie's mother and grandmother were true caregivers. They mended pockets and pants, sewed buttons, and darned socks. There wasn't any extra money to put toward clothes and frivolous purchases. His pants were already patched once. He figured one of them would wash the bloodstains out before putting them through the washer. They would line dry overnight, and if the humidity was low, they would be ready to mend in the morning.

Cara, Willie's mom, was an early riser and prided herself on her own appearance in addition to her children and home. As a young woman who won beauty pageants in her youth, her dresser back in Sacramento acted as a vanity with an oversized mirror for her wide array of rouge, eyeshadow, liners, and lipsticks. Hairspray held her hair in place when she put it in a bouffant for Sunday service, and when she left the house to go to the grocery store. She was a refined woman who exemplified dignity and grace.

She took great care when laundering and mending her husband's uniforms before the break of dawn, and always had the boys' play clothes ready by the time they came home after school. But she now lived in the country, and nobody cared about that.

In Willie's mind, his mother would have his pants ready to go by morning, at which time his father would need him to work on the farm and ready the house they were moving into. *I'll probably get paint on 'em,* he thought. He didn't mind helping and enjoyed the newness of the move. His father spent ten hours at work and was in the barn before Willie woke up. The man's excitement was evident, as was the joy his grandparents felt. But his mother was hit hard by the move and lifestyle changes that came with living in the country.

The magazines were not an accurate depiction of life outside the city. There were no supermarkets or malls. No cafés, boutiques, or sewing shops were near their small farm. The biggest store was a fruit stand where the owners had hundreds of acres filled with peaches. They sold fruit in the basement of the building where the outside temperatures were kept at bay. A forty-minute drive to the grocery for milk was out of the question.

Within the year, more people purchased the subdivided parcels and formed a co-op for food sources.

Most of the people from the city moved onto ten-acre parcels, where they participated in the sustainability project. One family kept a dairy cow, and the milk was shared with all the people who joined. Another had seventy-five tomato plants and a field of corn, while another kept beef cattle. The Collins household provided plums but had more acreage and was able to keep a few beef cows, chickens for eggs and meat, and a large vegetable garden. It took a lot of work to tend, and the boys learned to split chores. In the morning, they tended to the animals, collected eggs, and checked the garden for ripe pickings. After school, they went to the field, building fences, picking up where they left off the day before.

In less than nine months, they were moved into their new humble square house with its original handmade stairs, wooden shelves, and gas stove. The fireplace in the living room burned wood, and an old carpet William Sr. received as a gift from a retiring chief served as a floor covering. The boys had three small rooms to split while their parents had their own. To Willie, the house was monstrous. It was larger than the row house, and unspeakably larger than Baxter's trailer. It was similar in size and shape to his grandparents' house, which astonished him. However, realistically, it was a very simple, humble farmhouse that was barely big enough to house the family. As he explained to Eddie one day on their way to meet Dwayne after church, "I don't think Grandma and Grandpa even live in their house. What do they need with all that space now that we're gone?"

Eddie sighed. "I think they just like peace and knowing they have the room to entertain. It wasn't like that back in Sacramento."

Willie was twelve and maturing. He looked at life in a different way. The day he was chased by the cow and shot at by Baxter was the start of his personal journey. He wondered why anyone wanted to be such an unlikeable person. No one ever visited the man or brought him food. The people from his co-op passed around old clothes and found anything anyone needed if they made it known. All Willie knew was at least he didn't have to milk the co-op cow, but instead tended to the orchard, pastures, chickens, and beef cows.

He really started to pay attention when he realized that in less than two years, he could get a job. It was important to his father that he get his own bank account and save for the future. Willie's plan was to supplement his father's income. His father's paychecks came once a month, and on those nights, Cara took to fixing tuna covered in a homemade cream gravy and served it on toast. The boys didn't complain, and Willie looked forward to those dinners, but he understood why they ate what they did, when they did. He also knew the financial stress aged his parents. But they were happy because money didn't mean anything and wealth was not something the Collins family sought.

The mother he once knew—with the dyed hair, makeup, and hairspray—turned into a natural beauty like the other women in the area. His friends' mothers wore old dresses, skirts, or jeans. They pulled their hair back in a ponytail or wore it high in a bob. They didn't wear much makeup, and they lived to keep the house and family in order. The same went for the girls in school.

Not more than a stone's throw from Spence's house, Willie and Eddie learned of a girl named Dharma. She was the only girl, which meant she had every guy's attention. She was a brunette with streaks of red gold and eyes the color of the bluest sky. Willie especially liked her freckles. Her rosy lips and tomboy attitude made her extra special. The girls in his class were, "More like girls," he once told Eddie.

Over the school year, Willie noticed Eddie was quiet. He discovered his brother had a girlfriend he left in Sacramento and worried that there weren't any girls in the country. Willie couldn't blame him. After all, they only met Dwayne, Spence, and Pat that first week.

Later that year, on a weekend excursion to the mines, the boys all heard what sounded like girls laughing. They were at Spence's house and ran through the hayfield to find two girls swimming in the watering hole at the edge of the woods. They stood there watching for a spell, until Dharma caught a glimpse of them.

"Hey boys," she called.

Willie, Spence, and Pat turned around to avoid seeing them. Dwayne waved while Eddie returned their call.

"Hey," he said. Willie was impressed because he sounded cool and collected. His own heart thudded in his chest. There were girls in what he considered their backyard. They had crawled, climbed, swam, and scoured every inch of that mountain, and not once did they see a girl.

"Join us," the other girl hollered.

That's all it took for Dwayne and Eddie. They tore their shirts off and ran down the hill to meet the girls. Willie, Spence, and Pat stayed behind.

"Forget them," Spence said. "That's just Dharma's cousin, Jane."

Willie popped up to see what had happened. Eddie and Dwayne were getting splashed by the girls. "I'm not going down there."

"Me neither," Pat said. "Let's just go. They know where we'll be."

Willie nodded in agreement. "I've got the lights."

That was all the group needed. They gathered up their gear and headed to the mines. Willie glanced back at his brother. He knew wild horses wouldn't drag him away if girls were involved. He spit on the ground and set out after Pat and Spence. The three didn't talk much until they reached the loose board.

"Kinda strange not having those two knuckleheads with us," Pat said.

"Agreed," Willie said. He pulled out his light and turned it on. "It doesn't matter. We have tunnels to scout."

Spence pulled out his own light and led the way. Willie was used to Eddie looking out for him, and he for Eddie. His stomach groaned with angst over being responsible for himself, and a bit of guilt crept in for leaving his brother behind. Not that he thought Eddie wasn't enjoying his time, it was more for the brother code. It felt wrong. He put the negative thoughts aside, focused on finding new things, and how he could share those things with Eddie.

Pat kept up the rear. His flashlight pointed at Willie's feet. The way they walked; each boy illuminated the path for the one in front of him. A single file line down the center of the tracks. The wooden ties were snapped in some places. In others, they were loose from the rails. Though the rails were rusted, they were solid. Rot hadn't gripped them, only time and the humid air trapped in the cold, dark chambers.

"Which way today, boys?" Spence called back.

"I say, right," Willie said.

Pat pointed his flashlight to the right hand tunnel. "Right it is."

"You've never seen gold down here, for real?" Willie asked.

Spence laughed. "Nope. I find a piece of gold; I won't be wearing these trousers anymore."

"If I find gold, I'm going to put it in the bank and build on it. There are no pants worth giving up gold for," Willie said. Like the other boys, Willie and his family were penny pinchers who rarely, if ever, spent money on anything but necessities.

The two boys agreed and marched onward. The descent was sharp, but they knew that. It was Willie's favorite tunnel, so they went that way at least five times before. It was also why Willie chose to go there. He knew the tunnel well, and Eddie knew it was Willie's favorite, so he'd know where to find him if he decided to leave the watering hole.

"Careful," Spence called back. "This is the ledge. You got a foot to scale, or it'll be your death."

Willie understood. The ledge they walked on was a mere foot wide with a sudden drop of at least forty feet, according to Dwayne. He also told them that there were probably bodies down there, if not at the end, where the cavern filled with water. Willie didn't believe much of what came out of Dwayne's mouth, like the fact that Baxter shot at kids, but he did believe a body could be hidden in the tunnels. Willie agreed that the pitch-black recesses were perfect for getting away with murder. He just hoped not to run into any gangsters while he was in there.

Spence was older than Willie and Pat by a year. His legs were longer, and his torso had broadened from the previous summer. Willie took two shuffling steps to match one of their leader's. "Hey, slow down," Willie yelled.

"Hurry up, then," Spence said.

Pat poked Willie's back, "I don't want to be left here. Get moving."

Willie tried to go faster, but the damp air got to his batteries. His flashlight went dark, leaving him and Pat with one pale yellow halo.

"Uh, Spence," Pat called. "We got trouble."

Spence didn't answer, and they couldn't see his light.

"Spence," the two boys yelled together.

Still no answer.

"Here, give me your light. I'll see if I can fix it. Hold mine," Pat said. He took Willie's flashlight and handed over his own. Willie kept it shining on the end for Pat to see as he unscrewed the top. He slid out the batteries and put them back in after swapping their positions. Willie felt a shimmer of hope when he saw the bulb flicker as Pat screwed it back together, but then there was nothing.

"What do we do now?" Willie asked, trying not to let his voice show the rise in agitation swelling in his gut.

"We should go back out the way we came while mine still works. But we can't leave Spence alone," Pat said.

"Then we wait," Willie said, as he noticed Pat's flashlight growing dimmer.

5
PATIENCE

Willie's heart thudded in his chest. He plastered his back to the mine wall. The last thing he wanted was to fall into the black abyss. Pat's flashlight blinked twice, once, then nothing. The older boy smacked the flashlight against his thigh.

Nothing.

"I know we should wait for Spence," Pat said. "But I'm not sure how long we can stand here."

Willie thought back to when he heard his father talking with his grandfather about a case he had. It was several months before the big move. He mentioned that many times people went missing, and no one had a clue as to when or where they had gone. His father made sure to tell his boys that in times of trouble, they should focus.

That night, Willie asked his father, "What do you mean by focus?" It was a question that brought advice Willie would not forget.

"Because, in the end there is no such thing as impossible. You need a positive mental attitude. One that lets you think for yourself." William Sr. sipped his hot tea and looked at Willie, who was listening intently to his father's words. "You remember that, boy. Positive mental attitude. If not, you'll let things control your life instead of you controlling the problem. Never stop getting ahead."

William Sr.'s words replayed in Willie's mind as the silence closed in on him. What would get them to safety without leaving Spence? What was to say Spence's flashlight wasn't also on the fritz? At twelve, Willie knew he wasn't a young kid needing a rescue. He was smarter than that.

"Hey, Pat," he said.

"Yeah?" Pat answered, his voice soft.

"This is what we're gonna do." Willie unfurled his plan, which would give him the thinking room he needed and provide a solution to their current dilemma. "We know the ledge is narrow, but that's only like two hundred feet back. Then the tracks start up in the tunnel's interchange. You'll have to start first, but we can shimmy to the interchange. Once you feel the opening, we're safe and we can wait for Spence."

"That's good, Willie. Right smart of you."

Willie nodded, but Pat couldn't see it. "We'll keep talking so we know that we haven't lost contact. Go slow, and I'll follow."

"I'm stepping off," Pat said.

The boys reached the interchange. Willie felt the difference between the narrow pass and the cavernous enclosure. It was like the floor expanded into a room large enough to fit a small truck. Though the boys had explored several other mines in the area, this one had the largest tunnels.

Dozens of tunnels lead underground to where the mines were flooded when they no longer proved fruitful. The mine where Pat and Willie found their refuge was at an interchange that had collapsed tunnels. It produced caverns and blocked pathways. It was also the reason their parents warned them to stay out of the mines, as they were dangerous.

Willie and the boys were on their way to a flooded tunnel when the flashlights quit. Most of the tunnels had no tracks. Rock covered the walls and ceilings; the floor a mix of loose stone that fell over the years and dirt. Fine dust from the excavation process settled, and the smell of stagnant water permeated the air in places.

Pat called Willie to where he sat on the tunnel floor. "That was good thinking, Willie."

"Thanks," Willie said. It was the first time Willie realized the importance of stepping back to examine the situation to come up with a solution that mattered. He would draw on the day the lights went out as a means of proving to himself that nothing was impossible.

Just as the boys were settled, they heard Spence's voice. He wasn't calling them, but instead yelling. Willie couldn't make out what he was saying, but he knew it wasn't good. He saw the glow of Spence's flashlight round the bend on the narrow pass and then it illuminated the interchange.

Spence rushed past Pat and Willie. "Come on, let's get out of here."

Pat was hot on his heels. "What's got you so spooked?"

"D-dead man," Spence sputtered. The light at the end of the tunnel showed that they were close to the opening. Spence ran full on with Pat and Willie not far behind. Light hurt Willie's eyes, but even through his squints, he could see Spence's face.

"You're pale as a ghost," he teased.

"Don't say that. You don't know what you're talkin' bout," Spence coughed. He laid back on the gravel roadway. "There's a body. Back inside. I saw it."

Pat spit in the dry grass. "Enough, you're not pullin' my leg."

"I swear, Pat," he huffed. "Will, I shined my light in the water and there it was. A face staring up at me. It was floating, all bloated." He rolled over to his side, coughing.

Willie sat on the ground beside him. "You think he's been there long?"

"Don't know. Maybe he was put there," Spence said.

Pat went back to the entrance with Spence's flashlight. "Well, I want to see. I don't believe you."

"You can if you want," Spence said.

Willie scrambled to his feet. "Pat wait," he yelled,

not meaning to raise his voice as much as he had. "We just had our own dilemma. Spence went all the way and back with one set of batteries. What if his light gives out? Then what? We got nothing to come find you. Think smart." He stared his friend in the eyes, appealing to his common sense, praying his friend would listen and go back another day when they all had working lights and backup batteries.

Pat frowned and tossed the flashlight to Spence. "Fine, but it's not fair. He probably won't be there, next time."

"Why? You think he's gonna just walk outta there?" Spence asked.

Pat stuck his hands in his pockets and started the trek back to Dharma's house. "Come on."

When the boys reached Dharma's, Eddie and Dwayne were drinking lemonade in her yard. They had a small wooden table made of plywood on a stump. The girls sat on folding lawn chairs having changed into sundresses. Willie thought Dharma was one of the prettiest girls he'd ever seen. She wore a pink dress that reflected on her cheeks. Her naturally long black eyelashes accented her blue eyes and made his voice catch.

"You want some lemonade, Willie?" she asked.

"Uh, thank you," he said.

Dharma handed him a paper cup with a very pale liquid. "Here."

Willie took the cup and swallowed the contents in one gulp. He was thirstier than he realized after the morning's adventure into the mine and the long hike back. After he swallowed, the taste hit him. It was water with some sense of sugar, but almost no lemon. "That was great, thanks," he lied.

Dharma smiled and went back to sit in her place by the table. Her cousin had a paper cup too and stared into the liquid. Both girls giggled.

Pat and Spence sat in the grass by Eddie and Dwayne, but Willie was eager to get home. He was hungry, thirsty, and looking forward to his grandmother's cooking. Not to mention he kept thinking about the dead guy and how he got there. He also wanted to tell Eddie what happened, but he thought it was inappropriate to mention in front of the two girls.

"Guess what," Spence said after a second cup of lemonade. "I think I saw a dead body."

Willie clenched his fists. He wanted to be the one to tell his brother about Spence's claim to determine if it was true. He still didn't believe him and wanted proof.

"No way," Dharma said, putting her cup on the table.

"Yeah," Spence said, leaning back in the grass.

"Well, what did he look like?" Eddie asked, glancing at Willie. Willie shrugged, and Eddie nodded.

"Dead," Spence said. "He was drowned. Floating way back, in the bottom of the tunnel."

Dwayne threw a stick at him. "How we know you ain't pullin' our chain?"

"Because I saw it. I ain't goin' back there anytime soon. You three can go if you want, but I'll wait up top." He threw the stick back at Dwayne. "I wouldn't lie about something like that. It ain't right."

Willie studied Spence's face. The boy didn't appear to be lying. He was used to them laughing at him, but Spence's actions were different. Willie thought maybe it was true. He'd never seen Spence be so quiet. "I gotta get back," Dwayne said, hopping up and breaking the silence. "I got night chores before Ma makes dinner. I don't want her to have to do them."

"Why can't your father do them?" Dharma's cousin asked. Dharma smacked her hand to keep her from talking.

Willie sat next to Eddie, giving Dwayne his attention. He knew the boy lived with his mother, but never had the nerve to ask why he never mentioned his father. He figured Dwayne would say when the time was right. And since that time seemed to be now, he offered his respect by staying attentive.

Dwayne leaned against a small pear tree in Dharma's yard and pulled one of the branches until he caught a green leaf in his fingers and let the branch go. He held the leaf, pulling the greenery from the stem in strips. "I had the best Pa. He and Ma started the farm before I was born. A hundred acres half-filled with sheep, the other with peaches. When Dad got cancer, I had to step up. Then he died a couple years ago, leaving me the man of the house. I make sure we get the stuff done that needs doing, and Ma takes care of what she can, but we had to sell the sheep to keep the farm. We have chickens now. I feed 'em, collect eggs and wash 'em, that sort of stuff. And she makes peaches every way you can imagine."

Dharma blinked away tears. Willie sat back in shock. He hadn't thought about why Dwayne had the patchwork clothes he did, and why he only mentioned his mother. He had a job at the orchard after school, which made it hard for him to join in the adventures Pat, Eddie, and Willie planned.

"I'm sorry, Dwayne," Dharma's cousin said.

Dwayne smiled. "It's alright. Ma and I get along."

Dharma changed the subject, "So how long have you been in the Collins Pack?"

"Collins Pack," Spence said. "I like it, but why'd you pick Collins?"

Dharma shrugged. "Because there are two of them and only one for each of you, silly."

Dwayne was the first to extend his gratitude to Dharma for her hospitality. The other boys followed suit and gave their thanks. They left the trailer by way of the dirt road, BB guns at their sides, and flashlights in their pockets. Once they dropped off Pat at his house, Eddie, Willie, and Dwayne stopped at Spence's. His father was cleaning rabbit cages while his mother was making dinner.

"Hey there, fellas," Spence's father called. The boys waved. "You wanna stay for dinner? We got plenty."

Spence turned to his three friends. "Why not? We haven't eaten a bite."

"Well," Dwayne said, glancing at the Collins boys. "I should get going."

Willie noticed the disappointment on both his friend's and father's faces. "We could stay for just a bit, right, Eddie?"

Eddie nodded. "Dwayne you should too."

"For a bit," Dwayne agreed.

Spence showed the boys to the barn, where they had a wall of rabbit cages. Each was clean, white or brown, and fed with fresh grass. "These are my dad's. They're his pride and joy."

Willie turned in time to witness Spence's father nuzzling one of the white bunnies in his arms. "Can I hold one?"

"Only my dad holds them. He's particular about his rabbits," Spence said.

The boys followed their friend inside to where Spence's mother was setting the table. They went to the bathroom to wash up, and Willie noticed how much dirt he had on him. He washed the best he could in the sink before coming out to let Spence have a go. Eddie and Dwayne were swimming with Dharma, so they were clean as a whistle—at least that's what they thought. But they were swimming in a dirty old mud-filled pond. The last thing Willie wanted was to leave a dirt trail in his friend's house. His grandmother and mother wouldn't have it, so he made sure to practice what he knew. If nothing else, he figured it was good manners.

"Why don't you boys have a seat and I'll bring the food over," Spence's mom said. Her voice had a cheerful ring to it. "I made potatoes for an appetizer. I was going to serve them as dessert, but we have company, so . . ."

Willie whispered to Eddie, "Potatoes for dessert?"

Eddie shrugged.

Dwayne sat by Spence while Eddie sat next to Spence's dad. Willie sat by the mom's seat. She brought over the casserole dish with the potatoes and passed it around. Each boy took a dollop.

"You're growing boys. You can take more than that," Spence's dad said.

Dwayne took another spoonful and passed the dish to Spence in time for the boy's mother to hand him a platter of sandwiches. He took one and passed the plate. "Thank you. It looks great."

"Oh, you're too kind," she said. "If you boys want more Miracle Whip, just say the word."

Willie shot a look to Eddie, who returned the horror in his eyes. Willie hated Miracle Whip. He dreaded eating the sandwiches because of the Miracle Whip, but he took one as he knew he should and put it on his plate. "Thank you, ma'am."

"Don't be shy, eat," Spence said, halfway through his first sandwich.

Dwayne was finishing his while Eddie nibbled the edges of his. Willie was still working on the potatoes, trying to devise a plan to get out of eating the Miracle Whip. He noticed a sliver of meat inside that looked like dark turkey meat. "What kind of meat is it?" he asked, picking up it up to take his first bite.

Spence's dad, who had a blob of Miracle Whip squeezing from his sandwich, replied, "Rabbit."

At first, Willie thought he was joking. "Really?"

"Yup," Spence's mom replied.

Willie stared at Eddie, who was focused on his plate and working on the crust. He knew his brother was trying to find a way to make it seem like he had eaten the sandwich and would feign being full. He wasn't that adept at the art of deception, but he had to try. When the father reached for another sandwich and his mother was in the kitchen bringing back another tray, Willie tucked the sandwich in his sleeve.

"May I be excused?" he asked. "To go to the bathroom."

"Of course, dear," Spence's mom said.

Willie kept his arm out of it and walked to the bathroom. Once inside, he tore the sandwich to bits and discarded it in the toilet. "There is no way I'm eating one of those fluffy bunnies." He heaved over the toilet, the potatoes making their way up when he thought about Spence's father killing and skinning those little critters. "Nope, not gonna happen." He flushed the toilet and washed the Miracle Whip from his hands before heading back to the table. When he returned, there was a fresh sandwich waiting on his plate.

"I had Ma give you another since you were so hungry, Willie," Spence said.

Willie's heart dropped. How would he get out of eating the fuzzy bunny now? Eddie smiled at him. "Eddie, you were really hungry, too. Do you want to share?"

Spence handed the new platter of sandwiches to Eddie. "You can have more, too."

Eddie squinted at Willie as he took another sandwich. Willie smiled when he took a bite of his crust. There was no way he was going to force himself to eat the bunny while his brother got off free. As he was about to bite another side, the phone rang. Spence's mom handed Eddie the phone.

"Hello?" Eddie said. There was a loud voice, and then Eddie hung up.

"What happened?" Willie asked.

"We forgot to call Mom. They were expecting us home. We have to leave right away," Eddie said. "I'm so sorry to eat and run."

"Nonsense, you get home. We'll see you next time," Spence's dad said.

"Thank you for dinner," Willie called back as they ran out the door.

Both boys were praising their luck at not having to actually eat the rabbit meat or endure the Miracle Whip. When they returned home, their father was waiting with the willow branch. Willie knew there would be consequences for his actions, but he considered it a win. He would take the lashing because it meant he didn't have to eat the bunny sandwich. It was the first time he faced a punishment, happy to be there.

That day, Willie learned the importance of rules, using his head, and paying attention to the guidance his father was teaching him. The incident in the mine showed him how to remain focused on the moment and not lose his head. Learning about Dwayne's father made him realize how lucky he was. And to top it off, he realized how sometimes one needed a reminder of the rules of life, even if it was painful, it was a gift.

6
WILLIAM "WILLIE" COLLINS

William Collins Jr. was a curious, fun-loving, adventurous boy, who was willing to take on the world. It was in his nature to explore. He was also a gentleman, because he was taught the core values of life: hard work and determination with a splash of manners. His first year in his new home offered him a life that gave him insight into life outside the city. He realized the city was only a small piece of the world.

There was no rushing unless it was to finish the chores. There were no trolleys, few paved roads, and the homes were trailers and small farmhouses. Architecture took on a different meaning in the country. It was to provide a safe dwelling from the elements. Kids got whooped by their parents to keep them in line, and still they went on, taking over jobs at home when a parent fell ill, or passed away. Willie was no exception. His father worked hard. He was a cop and got paid monthly. His family always had to stretch their food and budget.

Some families didn't have enough money for a budget. They robbed Peter to pay Paul, as the saying goes. They raised their own food, or they didn't eat. It was a different life altogether. Willie hadn't realized people lived like that until his big move. It was eye-opening. But his young age made him impressionable. He was able to remember it all. The life in the city, the move to the country, and all the happenings that came with growing up.

After two years in the country, Willie became a young man. A teenager with drive and purpose. In fact, it was at that time his father taught the boys to drive. William Sr. found an old blue Chevy pickup truck with the shifter on the column. Willie learned to push in the clutch and brake at the same time to start the long-bed beast. He also learned that if you wanted to stop and keep the truck running, you had to do clutch first, then brake. To continue, you had to be in first gear, release the clutch until it grabbed halfway, before letting go of the brake and pressing the accelerator.

To Willie, it became second nature. He'd run across the yard, hop in, and start her up, then drive hay to the barn and to people who needed it. He used it to pull the old junk pile piece by piece, to the side of the yard. At least the heaviest metal parts, like the old clunky blades. His father made him and his brothers sort and stack the smaller tools neatly in the barn. He built a wooden shelf for them. They put rusted screws, bolts, and nails in separate mason jars, lined screwdrivers and wrenches in rows, and hung two sickles that he and Eddie assumed were from the 1800s.

Back in the 1800s, wheat was a huge part of California's history. The grain industry flourished because of the dry, hot summers and mild winters that brought plenty of rain to the region. Thousands of acres were dedicated to the crop, per farming establishment. This resulted in stripping the soil of essential nutrients that caused the wheat industry to falter and fail. Orange, peach, and plum orchards were introduced as another means of agricultural revenue, while farmland was split into smaller units. So, when Willie moved to the country, his glimpse into the past during classroom history became his life. Not only was California known for its grain production, but for the orchards, vineyards, and cotton.

By his fifteenth birthday, Willie had two years under his belt as a harvest boy at one of California's largest peach and plum producers, Verga Orchards. The fruit trees were part of an innovative practice set in motion because of the grain issues of the earlier century. During this time, he learned the difference between the clingstone and freestone. There were Red Haven, O'Henry, Fay Elberta, and Babcock, all with beautiful blossoms that filled the orchards with amazing scents in the spring and the smell of fruit in the summer. This was where a boy learned to work long, hard days—a ten-to-twelve-hour day was the norm.

All the boys worked on the farms, but Willie took his

job to heart, never missing a day. He moved ladders, set up bins, and harvested the fruits as fast as any migrant worker. In Willie's day, migrant workers were people who used to go from farm to farm, picking fruits from the trees. They often traveled by bus and lived in poor, temporary housing. He formed bonds with the people, learning about different cultures. He was a good-hearted young man. And the owners took notice. Willie could pick fruit as well as a veteran migrant worker.

"Hey, Willie," Jack called from the main house.

"Coming!" Willie put the bushel of O'Henrys that he was carrying to the farm stand in the basement at the side of the house. He was careful not to set it in the path of foot traffic, with all the workers and customers coming and going. It was the first Saturday in July. He had on a pair of denim overalls and suspenders. The sweat beaded on his forehead. He pulled the tail of his shirt up and wiped away the perspiration before jogging off to see what his boss wanted.

He got up there, ready to take on another duty.

Jack met him at the stairs with a glass of lemonade. "You work hard, young man," he started.

"Thank you, sir," Willie said, taking the glass offered, gulping at the cold sweet glass of liquid gold. At that moment, Willie would swear it was worth more than money.

"Don't think what you're doing goes unnoticed. I've

been watching you, granted I watch everybody, but you in particular. I like the way you work, Willie. You have a system and it's consistent. It doesn't matter if you're picking peaches, plums, zucchini, eggplants, cucumbers, or tomatoes. You get in there and do what needs doin', no hesitation. I like that." The tall, dark-haired Portuguese man swigged his own lemonade. "The customers noticed too. You carry armloads for the people. That makes them happy, which makes me happy. You see, Willie, I'm a businessman. Verga Orchards supplies this country with fresh produce every year. As long as the weather conditions are consistent, and the soil fertile, the fruits will grow, and the people will come to pick them. But customer service is invaluable in business. Relationships are built through repeat customers and quality service. Kids your age, what are you, fifteen—sixteen?" He looked at Willie, who was already five feet nine inches.

"Fifteen, sir," Willie said.

"Oh, you're a tall boy, Collins. Anyway, you make people happy, and that makes me proud to have such a good boy under my employ. What I'm getting at is that boys your age aren't always reliable. Heck, I'd say near all of em'. But you are like clockwork. I can count on you, Willie."

Willie sipped at the melting ice. Not knowing how to respond, he nodded.

"I'm promoting you," Jack said.

Willie smiled widely, trying to suppress his excitement. "Thank you, sir. What do you want me to do?"

"I'm making you a part-time fixture in the farm stand with some work in the fields. The bushels are heavy, and the baskets need collecting. You'll have to be on your toes, running fresh produce down and carrying orders out. I have no doubt you will continue with that work ethic of yours. You're a smart kid, and I know you'll continue working hard. And at the end of the week, whatever overripe peaches that are left, you can take your pickings of them. Enjoy them, because we're closed on Sunday, and by Monday, they'll be wasted."

"Thank you so much, sir! I won't let you down." Willie hurried back down to the house where the farm stand was, picking up another bushel to deliver, his heart bursting with pride.

That night, he went home with his own bushel of fresh peaches of all kinds. His father, mother, and brothers were outside on the porch. The white paint on the house reminded Willie of the pictures he'd seen in his mother's magazines. It was a true farmhouse with the purple and yellow plums hanging on the deep green trees behind the old beaten barn. He appreciated his country life more than before. Perhaps because he was recognized for his determination, or perhaps it was because he couldn't wait to share the bounty he hauled home.

His father stepped down to meet him. "Whatcha got there, boy?"

"A whole bushel Mr. Verga said I could have," Willie boasted. "I got a promotion."

William Sr. patted Willie on the back. "Really, what to?"

"Farm stand," Willie said.

It was enough for his father. They all went inside; Willie to wash up for dinner, Cara to wash the peaches, and William Sr. to sit at the table going over the bills. Willie came down in time to see Eddie walk through the door. His brothers washed their hands and took their seats around the table. Cara brought over a large bowl with Willie's first batch.

The peaches were soft, overripe, and extra sweet. His mother served them washed and diced into bowls with sugar and fresh milk from the co-op cow. Maybe Willie was biased because he'd earned them, but he swore they were the best peaches he'd ever eaten.

7
RESPONSIBILITY

O ver the last few years, Willie helped with the planting and harvesting of the peaches at Verga Orchards. He worked long hours, often starting at sunrise and finishing well after sunset. But he loved the work, and he enjoyed the camaraderie of the other workers on the farm. He remembered his first summer there and how his supervisor, Jack, taught him everything he knew.

It promised to be a hot, sunny day, and Jack had taken Willie and several other farmhands to a plot that needed to be cleared. They were going to plant a new row of peach trees in the coming winter. Willie thought it was odd—to plant trees in the winter—since they were all gathered right there, ready to work, why not plant the trees right now?

"If you need more hands, I'm happy to help," Willie offered, believing the reason behind Jack's apprehension to plant the trees was because of a lack of workers.

Jack took him aside and started to explain the process of peach tree planting. "Well, Willie," he said, "peach trees differ from other fruit trees. They need to be planted in the winter, while they are dormant. By doing this, the trees can establish a strong root system in well-draining soil before the growing season begins in the spring."

Willie gave Jack his full attention. The more Jack explained the process of planting peach trees, the more Willie wanted to retain. He loved the fragrance that filled the spring air when the pink and white blossoms covered the hundreds of acres across the hilltops. Willie learned about the different types of peaches and how they were grafted onto the rootstock to create new trees. He also learned about the importance of pruning excess blossomed branches from the trees. A second pruning took place once the residual limbs bore fruit. By thinning the fruit from the limbs, it afforded the existing peaches the nutrients necessary to make a plentiful and healthy harvest.

As the summer wore on, Willie worked hard on the farm, helping to tend to the trees and harvest the ripened fruit. He learned about the difference between clingstone peaches that were used for canning to the freestone peaches that were sold fresh at the market. He even got to taste some of the new varieties, such as the sweet and sour Elberta peaches. The different flavors and textures of the peaches fascinated Willie, and he started to think of one day owning his own peach orchard, though his family had a small plum farm.

Willie's father had encouraged him to get a summer job to help him save up for college. But Willie already planned to apply to Verga Orchards since the idea of summer work was brought to his attention. He learned about agriculture from his family's small gentleman's farm and thought about the benefits he would bring home from his knowledge: working for one of the largest fruit orchard employers in Northern California. Little did he know that this summer job would turn into a passion he would pursue for years to come.

Now that he was fifteen, Willie looked forward to his new position in the farm market. He already knew the ladies who worked in the basement where the fruits and vegetables were kept cool. Having his hard work recognized by Jack and the ladies in the market made Willie's morning journey to the farm that much better. He couldn't help but admire the beauty of the orchard. Rows of peach trees stretched out before him, each one laden with golden ripe fruit just waiting to be harvested. Willie had always loved peaches, but he never appreciated just how much work went into growing them.

As he walked up the dirt driveway at the farm, he saw Jack waiting. He was a shorter man in his late sixties, with dark black hair combed over neatly. The man was in charge and one of the owners. And now that Willie was going to work with the public, he figured Jack would want to see that he understood his new position. Willie hoped to be a man who oversaw a successful production one day, much like Jack.

"Good morning, Willie," Jack said, smiling. The sun caused sweat to gather on the man's thick black eyebrows—they were messy. He wiped it away with his wrist. "Ready for another day of work?"

"Yes, sir," Willie replied, eager to undertake his new position.

"Good to hear, young man." He waved for Willie to follow him to the barn where bushels of Elbertas, tomatoes, and strawberries awaited. "There's the tractor. Just load up the bins and head over to the market. Betty and the girls are already setting up. Why don't you go check in with them?" Jack strode off, whistling toward the main house that served as his office.

Willie was taken aback at first, because he thought Jack would provide more direction. He understood the basics of the new position, but he had questions. He hadn't gone to the market with the tractor and wasn't sure if he was expected to load the trailer multiple times, or even if he was to return during the day for more produce to bring down. Jack told him to help the ladies and carry products for the customers. The more he thought about it, the more he realized Jack trusted Willie's judgment and character.

It was a moment of realization for Willie. He was trusted, and it was up to him to make decisions that would best serve the farm market and keep the customers happy.

As the workday wound down, Willie felt a sense of satisfaction wash over him. He worked hard and learned a lot, and he knew he was one step closer to his dream of owning a peach orchard of his own someday. Over the next few weeks, Willie developed a talent for spotting the ripe unblemished fruits from the ones used for canning, baking, and cooking. He was always eager to lend a hand whenever it was needed, and he loved being trusted. He was proud of his accomplishments.

Summer was winding down, and Willie had grown another two inches. He was tall and lanky, with a mop of curly brown hair and a farmer's tan. He was strong from the farm labor, lifting baskets and bushels. He was also on the local school basketball team, and though he wasn't as good at it, he loved baseball. He even enjoyed a game with his friends: Dwayne, Pat, Spence, and his older brother Eddie, though Eddie was heading to college in the fall. They made his last free spring the best of their teenage years.

Willie pitched against Spence and Pat while Eddie refereed, and Dwayne took the field. Unlike the manicured ball fields back in Sacramento, the field in town was a patch of dried dirt and sun-parched grasses. They used large stones and sticks as base markers while Willie provided the mitts and bat. Pat had a ball from when his father played catch with him, before his passing.

Baseball was a big deal in their small town. The games,

referred to as pickup games, were reminiscent of those when Willie would dash out to meet the city kids after school. But here, there were a handful of boys, and the teams were odd or even depending on the day, even with the field in the center of town. As he got older, Willie's skills on the field only grew. He was a natural at the game, with lightning-fast reflexes and a strong arm. And though Willie was known among them as a fast runner, he was building a reputation for himself as a pitcher.

One day, while Willie was practicing on the high school field, his coach approached him. Coach Sanchez was a stern, no-nonsense kind of guy, but he had Willie's respect. "Willie," he said, "I've been watching you play for a while, and you've got a hell of an arm. I won't even comment on your aim."

Willie smiled; his heart quickened with pride at the compliment. He always looked up to the coaches during his school career and hearing him say that meant his practices were paying off. Sometimes it seemed like the coaches were only interested in his basketball skills.

"So," the coach continued, "I've been thinking. You're not just good at baseball, you're a natural athlete. Have you ever thought about trying out for the track and field team? You've got speed, agility, and strength. You'd be great at the shot put or the long jump. And who knows, maybe it'll even help you become a better ballplayer."

Willie's focus was always on basketball and baseball,

and the idea of trying something new excited him. He decided to stop in at the next track meet and see what it was all about. He enjoyed sports and knew, at times, that he missed the larger group of kids in Sacramento Park. The track team had both boys and girls at the meet. The baseball team was small because, as Willie knew well, the high school boys had year-round jobs and worked in their homes since many lived on family farms. Willie was not able to play football because the farms were busy during the summer and work was a priority over sports. Working part-time during the school year allowed him to play some sports.

The following day, Willie showed up at the track field. It was a half-mile gravel oval off the side of the baseball field with which he was already familiar. He also knew the track well because he was required to run a mile at the start of every school year since he was ten, which he hated. As he watched the track team stretching and jogging, a spark of excitement lit in his core. They were fast and strong, and he could feel the competitive spirit rise inside him. He would be good at this, too. And to make things even better, a familiar face jogged up to him.

"Hey, stranger," Dharma said. She had grown into the prettiest girl at school, at least that's what Willie thought. "What are you doing here?"

Willie ran his hand through his curls. "Branching out. I didn't know you ran."

"I've been on track since eighth grade. I sprint and do the long jump."

"Oh," he said, remembering the previous end-of-year's picnic. "That's right, you did the five-hundred-yard dash and the relay race. Blue ribbons I believe."

Dharma blushed, "Yup. I like running. It makes you feel free."

"I get that. Usually, I'm at work or doing homework, but I run when I'm playin' ball." He thought about the times he and his friends used to go to the mines and sit on top of the train tunnels. It seemed like the older they got, the sparser those excursions became. Just like running, he didn't realize how it was slipping. Those days made him feel free. He made a mental note to talk to the guys about getting together for a hike after work since he still had Saturday afternoons off. He knew Eddie would be in and probably Dwayne at the very least. "Hey, Dharma. Want to come to the mines sometime? Maybe Saturday evening? It'll be me and Eddie for sure."

"Oh, Willie. My cousin is visiting. You remember her?"

"Bring her. The more the merrier," he said, suppressing the thumping in his chest. He liked Dharma. She was the prettiest girl in the school and her accompanying them would make his year.

Dharma looked back at the coach, who was blowing the whistle, signaling for them to gather for the roll call.

"Alright, Willie. We'll see you then."

Willie's smile was so deep it hurt his face. He jogged after her to where the coach stood with the clipboard. It was a new feeling. Was it freedom? Or was it the realization that life had changed, and he had the power to control the direction?

That afternoon, Willie tried the hundred-yard dash, shot put, and the long jump. To his surprise, he found he was good at all of it and enjoyed it. His natural athleticism made it easy for him to pick up the techniques, and soon he was throwing the shotput farther than anyone else and jumping farther than he ever thought possible. He likened it to peach fights and pitching.

When Willie went home that evening, he felt a unique sensation in his legs. He was sore, but in a good way; the way that told him he was pushing himself to be the best he could be, and that was the feeling he loved. He was finding something new and winning. It was a feeling he recognized over the last year, and it seemed to grow. Little did he know that feeling was the beginning of a lifetime of rising above new challenges and excelling.

8
TRICKSTERS

Willie could hardly suppress the urge to run out the door. It was finally the day he waited for all week—hiking to the mines. He managed to get Eddie and Dwayne to come along on the day trip to the hills with Dharma. The fact that he hadn't eaten breakfast kept him from darting out into the warm spring breeze. It blew the yellow curtains from the window over the kitchen sink. The wind chime that hung on the porch played a high-pitched tune. Bacon grease permeated the air, causing his growing stomach to growl.

"Good morning, boys," his mother said, placing plates filled with three farm fresh eggs, two thick slices of toasted white bread, and a pile of bacon in front of them. She had already prepared a pitcher of orange juice and filled their glasses on the table. "Eat quick, don't dawdle, but chew your food."

Willie nodded. She didn't need to tell him twice. He wanted to get to work as soon as possible that Saturday because the sun went down at eight. He was also certain Eddie and Dwayne were feeling the angst too. When he told them about Dharma and her cousin joining them, both jumped at the opportunity. Pat and Spence grumbled because they both had tilling and sowing to do. Willie ate his food in record time, much like when he was younger and eager to run off with the guys.

Once Willie was finished, he took off to work. With afternoon plans pressing on his mind, the work at the orchard flew by. He wasted no time getting home, and when he did, he ran inside to change into blue jeans and a T-shirt with brown leather shoes. Willie stopped to comb his hair before running out to meet Eddie, who was already behind the house. Both were equipped a flashlight with fresh batteries, Tic Tacs, and a pellet gun slung over their shoulders with a tube of ammo. Willie added a slingshot to his back pocket.

"Which one do you like better?" Dwayne asked once they met up with him at the descent of the hill, just after Baxter's trailer.

"I dunno," Willie said. "I didn't talk much with Jane. I don't really know her." Willie knew full well he preferred Dharma, just like every other guy that went to their school. She had rosy, full lips that drew his attention every time she spoke.

Though they could be models, as Dwayne often said, "They're all natural beauties."

Eddie kicked a large stone into the woods. "I think they're both swell, but Dharma's the pretty one."

Dwayne whistled. "Well, guess it doesn't much

matter. We're going to see them both, and that's good enough for me."

The three boys made their way to Dharma's house. She and Jane were sitting on the front steps, waiting. They each wore denim jeans, but a different kind of flowered top. Dharma's was pink with white daisies while Jane had a yellow elastic top with blue periwinkles. They both had their own flashlights.

"Hey, boys," Jane said.

Dwayne stepped ahead of Willie and Eddie. "Hey."

Dharma sidled up to Willie. "It's exciting, going up there."

"That's why we go. You never know what you'll see," Willie said, winking his eye at Eddie. "You ever shoot a slingshot?"

"Uh, uh," Jane said.

Eddie cleared his throat. "Well, let's get going. We want to be able to get back before sundown. The summer sun hasn't hit yet, and it feels like the days are still not as long as the nights."

Willie raised his brow at his brother. "Yeah, okay."

The girls giggled.

Willie and his friends grew up exploring the mine country in the California hills. They knew the area like the back of their hands and often spent their Saturdays exploring the nearby trails, creeks, and mines even though they knew it was dangerous and shouldn't.

As the five teenagers set off on their hike, Willie couldn't help but feel a sense of freedom and adventure. The sun was shining, and the air was crisp and fresh. Maybe it was the fact that he was with his friends again, or maybe it was because he had two girls joining them. He felt confident and more aware of the landscape than usual. They followed the winding path that led them deeper into the wood line that led to the creek, and soon were surrounded by towering trees and the gentle rustling of leaves.

The two girls were not new to hiking, but Willie, Dwayne, and Eddie showed off their skills. They taught them how to spot animal tracks, identify different types of plants and trees, and how to use landmarks as markers to navigate the trails. The bright green leaves and granite outcrops formed patterns, at least in Willie's mind. He pointed out the various shapes and referred to the trees as 'ole slim' or 'big pine'. They were familiar and hadn't changed since he first learned to follow them. He referred to the crevices in the rock by their gaps and the peaks by height.

As they hiked, they came across a small creek that meandered through the forest at the base of the hill that led to the train tracks. The same stream where Willie and Eddie were told not to drink the water. They stopped to take a break, and Willie pulled out his homemade slingshot. He had spent hours crafting it out of a forked branch and some rubber bands, so he was eager to show it off to the girls.

Dharma and Jane were impressed by Willie's skills. He picked up small bits of stone and called out his target.

"See that hanging branch with the lone leaf? Watch." He pulled the bands back and let the stone fly. He hit the leaf with precision, and enough force to tear a hole in it.

"Can I try?" Dharma asked.

"Sure," Willie said, handing her the slingshot. He stood behind her, handed her a small stone from his pocket, and showed her how to load it. "Put in here and pull back as far as you can. Pick your target and line it up between the two points of the fork."

She aimed for the same branch and leaf. Then she let the elastic go; the stone fell three feet in front of her. They all laughed as they took turns shooting at rocks and twigs, but the girls grew bored and decided to explore the area around the stream.

Willie, Eddie, and Dwayne stayed behind testing their accuracy with the slingshot until they heard rustling in the bushes, higher up on the mount. Willie heard the whine and recognized the owner before it darted out into the clearing on the hill overlooking the stream where the girls were standing, ankle deep, completely unaware. Willie's heart thudded at the sight of the bobcat, but he grabbed a bigger stone, raised his slingshot, and aimed. He looked the wild cat in the eye and let the stone fly. It struck the rock below the animal.

Dwayne started waving his arms over his head. "Get outta here."

Dharma and Jane turned to look over their shoulders and froze.

Eddie grabbed his pellet gun and loaded the reservoir with the end of the barrel facing the ground before aiming at the creature. He cocked the lever and pulled the trigger. The pellet hit the ground above it. The hissing animal stepped back. Willie loaded the slingshot, pulled back, and released the plum-sized stone. It struck the ground in front of the animal's paw. Startled, the bobcat leapt away.

"I thought you guys were dead shots," Dwayne said. "You both missed."

Willie frowned at him. "The intention is not to kill or harm the animal, but to scare it away. You don't want an injured animal running around."

The boys' father had taught them about keeping the dangerous critters of the California mountains at bay. They had bobcats, cougars, coyotes, and rattlesnakes. He taught them that getting up close to the creature was better and more effective than striking it.

The incident raised Willie's anxiety for the rest of the hike, but it still didn't thwart their plans. Once the girls got to the mines, they wouldn't go in. Willie urged them, getting them to go a mere twenty feet in before they turned around and ran to the exit. They stood outside in the sunlight next to a patch of overgrown grass.

When Dharma and Jane stepped closer, they heard a rattle.

"Is that a rattlesnake?" Dharma asked, her face going white.

They all heard the sound again, and Jane screamed.

Willie pulled a small rectangular box from his pocket. "What? You want a Tic Tac?"

9
SLAUGHTER BALL

The school year arrived with Willie filled with pride. Between the promotion at work and the mine adventure with the girls, he was grateful for every moment and cherished his new memories. Just like the ones he had back when he was a newcomer in high school. It was the same time of year, early autumn, and he was being tested by the older, senior boys.

The first month of ninth grade, Willie had gone face-to-face with a kid named Stephen, who was the captain of the football team. He was a big six-foot, two-hundred-pound kid with muscle. The gym teacher set up the guidelines for slaughter ball; a game that involved two teams standing on opposite sides of the gymnasium. A center line was declared or marked with plastic cones and a number of volleyballs were lined up along that line.

That first game, Willie watched Stephen step up to the line, grab a ball, and throw it at top speed into the opposing players. The new freshmen were scared and ran to the back of the gym against the wall. He hit them in the gut and back. Stephen was pompous and stood on the line, even if he did not have a ball. When Willie was the last one left on his team, Stephen laughed. No one dared hit him with a ball.

"You're dead now, Freshman."

"That Collins kid is small and fast; makes a hard target," the gym teacher taunted.

Stephen pulled his arm back and let the ball fly. Willie ran past him, the ball missing his head by an inch. He came to a skidding halt. The ball struck the floor with enough force to cause an echo. Willie knew he'd meant for the ball to hurt. He grabbed the ball from the floor and whirled around. His foe stood in front of him, daring Willie to hit him with the ball.

Willie stepped up to the line. He understood Stephen was testing him. Willie held the ball in his hand and threw the ball the ball striking Stephen directly in the face causing his nose to swell. Then all hell broke loose for Willie, as the senior bully attacked him.

"I'm gonna kill you," Stephen said, clutching his bleeding nose.

Willie tripped him and landed on top. He punched Stephen in the gut after Stephen swung and connected with Willie's eye. He didn't dare try to get away. He tucked his head into Stephen's chest and threw a punch at his head. He connected, only to feel the blow come to the back of his own head. But Willie had Stephen down and was on top, using all his strength to keep him from getting up. Willie kneed him in the gut and hung onto his arms. The older boy struggled to free himself. In doing so, Willie's fist flew up to Stephen's chin. The fight went on, punch for punch, for ten minutes before the gym teacher put an end to the brawl.

"Oh man," Dwayne said. "It looked like you had him."

Willie sat back against the padded wall. "Maybe, but if it went on much longer, I think he would have killed me." Willie held a paper towel over his nose and pinched it until the blood dried.

That ninth-grade fight wasn't the first fight Willie had gotten into, and it wasn't the last.

Now, as an older teen in his second year of high school, Willie had an established rank among the upperclassmen. He was capable of holding his own. He was older and stronger. The same game was set up during winter recess, which excited him. He liked the rough nature of the sport. And now that he was bigger, he could block the younger or smaller kids from the bullies on the other side.

No matter his age, he always assisted the underdog. Though the bullies usually became congenial friends. As he told Dwayne, "At the end of the day, yeah, you will have bloody noses. But you have something bigger, more important."

"And what's that?" Dwayne asked.

"Respect." Willie said. He knew it to be true because it was how he felt when he approached the guys who started fights with him. It didn't matter who won, just that you fought for your purpose. You stand your ground, and stand up for the weak. "Perseverance is key." Willie's dad taught his boys to never start a fight, but never back down from one, no matter how big the bully.

Dwayne shook his head. "If you say so. I see it as a challenge."

"There are no hiccups in life, Dwayne, only challenges. I like challenges. They give me experience and help me grow. What fun would it be if we stood back, just taking life as it was handed? I want to stand up for something, meaning the underdog. And now, I need to move on."

"To what?"

"The coach thought I should try out for the basketball team."

***

Willie did, in fact, make the basketball team. It was no surprise that he was skilled in athletics with his baseball and track record. He was a good shot, but he was a better sprinter. Willie was fast and could dribble the ball quickly and effortlessly down the court. It was a talent he showed during slaughter ball and the one that caught the coach's attention. He was learning how skills often overlapped.

He knew that his speed in baseball helped him in track and vice versa. Then, using his ability to slide between bases, let him dodge the incoming ball. But he built a new skill. Grabbing the ball and slinging it back across the gymnasium and to his teammates. Basketball required coordination, strength, and agility. But it also required passing. A good passing guard keeps his teammates scoring. Willie was tall, thin, and aggressive. He wouldn't back down against an advancing team. He also knew how to jump, and for his height, he could really leap.

His muscles were conditioned for all the moves. He just needed to focus a little bit while dribbling the ball and shooting. The coach held practices every day for an hour and a half. He worked the players hard. They had to run exercises called *suicides* up and down the length of the gym and do dribbling drills. Dribbling drills were the hardest for Willie to grasp, but by the end of his first week, he was dribbling as well as the rest of the point guards.

Their first game, the cheerleaders came in, which Willie loved. He didn't really watch the games because he had obligations, but now that he was on the team, he devised a way to complete his personal responsibilities while fulfilling his obligation to the team.

The referee blew the whistle. The ball was tossed in the air and Willie's teammate slapped it. The ball went back into the opposition's side of the court. All the boys tussled to get to the other side, but Willie was already there. He took the ball and threw it to the team captain who scored the point with a short jump shot.

The spectators, mainly students and family, applauded. It was a modest sound but encouraged Willie even more. He liked proving himself and pushing to be the best he could be, no matter what the task. Having fun while doing it was a plus, and he enjoyed basketball. He liked playing with the team and the fast-paced game.

Squeaking sneakers and the sound of the ball slamming into the backboard over the hoop resounded in the room. The opposing team had taken a shot. The ball made its way around the rim and fell to the side. Willie's teammate jumped, grabbed the ball, and started dribbling down the court. One of the kids from the other team was crowding him. Willie leapt in front of him, put his arms up and out. The kid lost his advantage, which gave his teammate the opening he needed. He got two steps closer to the hoop and shot a high-arching shot that went in.

The cheerleaders shook their pompoms and chose the shooter's name to chant. Then Willie heard his name, but from the bleachers. Dharma and her friend Jill were in the bleachers. "Go, Willie!" Dharma yelled, clapping her hands. Jill clapped along with her.

Willie nodded in their direction and went back to his position at the top of the key, directing the traffic of the team. The game went on with Willie intervening all the opposition's attempts. He lunged, leapt, and swept the ball down the court. Willie immediately noticed his teammate was open for a *fast break*. Just as Willie was about to pass the ball, his teammate was knocked over by a player on the other team. Now Willie didn't have an opening. In that split second, he made the decision that would dictate his career that season. He stopped and took the shot from a relatively long distance.

The people in the bleachers stood. Dharma put her hands over her eyes. The cheerleaders clutched their pompoms. The referee waited with the whistle in his mouth. The ball hit the rim and teetered in. Willie scored. This was just the beginning of his success as an athlete at his high school.

Over the next couple of months, Willie watched the number of spectators grow. He'd unintentionally become the talk of the school. He had become the basketball star after being the high scorer in the last five games, helping his team to victory. His name was chanted by the cheerleaders and written on poster boards by fans sitting in the bleachers. The cheer captain often smiled and blew him a kiss at the start of the game after the first few weeks. Willie noticed a lot of girls started coming in to watch him play. They would call his name and then applaud louder whenever he made a basket.

The final game was a championship game. The game was at home and the cheerleaders were already chanting.

The coach gave the team a pep talk. "Willie, it's no

secret. We're counting on you." He paused, staring Willie in the eye. "This is the last game of the season and the biggest win. Guys, we just need to bring this home. You know the drill. You're the best team out there, now go prove it."

The whistle blew and the game was underway. The ball and scoring went back and forth between the teams. Willie had the ball, but it was swooped out from under his hand. He ran after the guy and grabbed it back. Another opponent took it, but Willie's teammate knocked it away. The ball was heading toward the side, out of bounds. Willie lunged for it, he grabbed it and threw it to another teammate who quickly turned and shot. It was good.

The game went on in the same manner. It was a tie, and the last shot of the evening was in Willie's hands. He was racing toward the hoop, stumbled on the opponent's foot, dropped the ball, but righted himself. He leapt toward his foe and, reaching down, swiped the ball. Not daring to take a chance at losing it again or worse, losing the game, Willie paused and started dribbling down the court. Just in time, his teammate set a screen allowing Willie to sprint for the basket and lay the ball up for the winning score just as the clock ticked to zero. The ball smacked the red square on the backboard and dropped in.

Cheers and applause echoed in the gymnasium. The coach slapped him on the back, and his teammates crowded around him. They won the championship because Willie made the final shot.

"Willie!" the head cheerleader called.

Willie left the guys for a moment, the smile on his face aching. The adrenaline was coursing through him. He jogged over to where the cheerleaders were gathering their poms. "What's up, Deb?" he exclaimed with a smile.

She clutched her pompoms to her chest. "Will you go to the Sadie Hawkins dance with me?"

The Sadie Hawkins dance was like a rite of passage to all the guys in school. It was a big deal because the girls had to ask the guys. If you weren't asked, then you were no one. Willie was elated to be asked by the head cheerleader, a beautiful young lady who looked as striking as her personality, and who was also two years his senior. "Yes, of course. I'd be honored."

Deb squealed, shook her pompoms, and kissed his cheek before running over to the rest of the girls. As Willie made his way back to the guys who were still standing on the court, he realized he was one lucky guy.

10
A PENNY SAVED

It was the summer Willie looked forward to for the last two years. He was sixteen. Verga Orchards was a daily routine of hard work and sweat. Every morning, he would wake up early, head out to the orchard, and start the tractor. He worked tirelessly to load the harvested crops in the shaded barn onto the trailer. Once he drove them to the farm stand, he unloaded them, repeating the process as inventory dictated. He was grateful for the job, grateful to be out of the scorching sun most of the time, and even more grateful for the joy he felt helping the customers. Willie felt a sense of freedom and independence knowing that his supervisor Jack and the ladies who tended to the stand trusted him. He had no one looking over his shoulder because they knew Willie would do what they needed without hesitation and often without needing to be asked.

He had to learn how to drive the tractor, back in a trailer, and maneuver around ruts and obstacles. Last winter over break, he asked Jack if he wanted help with the planting because he knew there were fewer migrant workers in the winter than in spring and summer. To

Willie's surprise, he found himself driving the tractor with a trailer of saplings waiting to be planted. He helped dig holes and secure the young plants, putting his all into each day. It also added to his desire to own his own peach trees. And if he wanted to be successful, he had to follow his father's sage advice, *"Doing is learning."*

William Sr. told him, *"There's no better teacher than experience."* It was a phrase he said when the boys were helping with new tasks around their own farm or, in Willie's case, when he went to help the other members of the co-op. In this way, Willie learned how to mend fences, put in irrigation, build a wheelchair ramp, and put gypsum on the studs of a framed house. He milked the community cow and collected eggs while learning what kinds of chickens grew fastest for food. Those would be the Cornish hens, Plymouth Rock chickens, and Rhode Island Reds. He learned how to drive the old truck with the tight steering and slipping clutch.

Life in the country had taught Willie a lifetime of lessons he would never see in a classroom. He learned how to hitch and unhitch the flatbed in record time. He was fast and proud. Because he was paid for these experiences, he took his earnings and saved. He put nearly every cent into his account, counting the days to when he turned sixteen and got his driver's license. But that wasn't all. Willie wanted to buy his own truck. All that saving led to him scouring classifieds in the Sunday newspaper.

For months, Willie circled ads. The money didn't come easy, and he wasn't about to let it go that way. All the boys in the area drove pickup trucks, and Willie was no different in what he desired. He wanted a truck he could take through the rugged terrain and one that could serve a purpose, after all, Willie had learned to drive on the ranch when he was fourteen. He decided to forgo the purchase because he had the truck he learned on, a long bed two-wheel drive 1967 Chevrolet blue pickup truck that had a *three on the tree* shifter. The *three on the tree* was a shifter located on the steering column. He and his brothers all learned to drive that truck on the dirt roads and sometimes without their parents' knowledge. When Willie was about fifteen, he and Eddie would take it on the old, winding, narrow country roads.

Willie also would drive around Verga Orchards. They had what they called a *jalopy*, and an old 1956 yellow pickup truck with the cab cut off. That also had the *three on the tree* shifter. Jack was shocked when he discovered Willie knew how to drive it at fourteen years old.

One day, when Willie was out driving a load of hay home, his youngest brother urged him to let him get behind the wheel. "I know how to shift. I'm fourteen now. You were my age when you learned."

Eddie was in the cab with them. He looked at Willie and shrugged. "Fine with me."

"I don't know. You sure you know what you're doing?"

Willie asked. He looked at his youngest brother's eager face. If nothing else, Willie would have a funny story to tell. He was certain the kid wouldn't get the beast home. Willie pulled over on the side of the road and let Stewart slide behind the wheel. "You have to push in the clutch and brake when you turn it over."

Stewart did as he was instructed.

"You gotta put it in first. Then ease off the clutch and press the gas," Willie said.

"I know," said Stewart. The young teen pulled the shifter toward him and pulled it down. He let off the brake, but let off the clutch too soon. The truck bucked and stalled.

Willie laughed. "I said press the gas."

Stewart tried again. This time the truck jumped forward as it continued to lurch. Willie held onto the door. His brother eased on the gas and maneuvered back onto the road. He pushed in the clutch and pressed the shifter forward and up. It didn't make it into second and he ground the gears. The sound of metal groaning made him wince.

Eddie held his ears. "You have to push the clutch to the floor before switching gears."

"I did," Stewart said, his voice higher pitched with excitement.

"You didn't, otherwise you wouldn't have ground the gears," Willie reasoned.

Stewart drove the truck in second gear up the hill and then shifted to third. "Yeah, I told ya, I could do it." He drove until the driveway to the ranch appeared.

Willie pointed to the clearing just before the rows of plum trees on the left. "Slow down or you'll miss it. You have to downshift."

The driveway was a rustic dirt pass between the pasture and plum orchard. It was narrow; just wide enough to fit one truck. The dust kicked up from the truck and wrapped around them. "Slow down," Willie repeated.

Stewart downshifted to second and turned the wheel hard to make the ninety-degree turn into the long, dirt road driveway. He pressed the brake when he turned for the first time, but he forgot to turn the wheel back after turning in.

"Turn, turn, turn," Eddie screamed.

It was too late.

All three boys yelled as Stewart took out their new fence and put the truck down into a three-foot ditch in the pasture. Willie laughed, followed by Eddie and Stewart.

"Eddie, you were so scared," Willie taunted.

"Was not. He needed to turn the wheel back," Eddie retorted.

Stewart hopped out of the truck. "No, you were scared. You should have heard yourself."

"Yeah, well, you need to steer," he said.

"Come on, I'll start the truck. You two push," Willie said.

The two boys got behind the truck and pushed when Willie gave it gas. They rocked the truck until it gained enough traction and momentum for Willie to ease it out onto the dirt and rock-filled driveway. The two boys hopped into the truck bed and Willie drove them the rest of the way home.

Later that summer, Eddie, who was eighteen then, was in his last year of high school. He had saved his money from working at different orchards over the past four years and decided he wanted a car of his own. He found a 1970 Camaro which Willie thought was cool, but Eddie wanted to make it his own.

"What are you doing?" Willie asked, watching Eddie tape brown paper bags over the windows, mirrors, and lights of the Camaro.

"Painting," Eddie said.

"Why?"

"Why not?"

"Because it's already cool."

"Well, I like orange," Eddie said. He took out orange spray paint and started on the roof with a sweeping motion. "Oh, yeah."

"Seriously?" Willie asked. "Orange?"

"Yup."

Over the course of Willie's teenage years, the pickup truck was the main mode of transportation. It had more appeal for farm boys and was reliable enough that they drove it for years. And when Eddie went off to college, Willie got to drive the ugly orange Camaro. Sixteen was a fun year and one that proved saving paid off.

In the country, Willie and the boys learned the value of life skills—many times the hard way. Hard, difficult work that most did not want to do, driving an old *jalopy* on the orchard and mastering the *three on the tree* taught Willie perseverance and judgment. These were experiences he would draw on later in his life when he had three ranches of his own and a collection of tractors and trucks. And the first two years at the orchard would impress on him the importance of passion, perseverance, and observation. Three skills that would prove necessary the following summer when he was seventeen.

11
EAGLE EYE

"**S**omething's not right," Willie said to Betty, the farm market supervisor.

"What do you mean? Is it school? You're going to be a junior now. It must be tough and exciting at the same time—knowing you only have two years left." The older woman blinked at him with kind, endearing eyes. She was tall with perfectly groomed gray hair in a bouffant. She was a sophisticated lady, with crippled fingers, but very glamorous. Her sister-in-law also worked in the stand. She was shorter, sort of plain-looking, and wore a pair of denim overalls with a yellow T-shirt. The two sisters ran the fruit stand business until their late sixties from the 1906 Victorian farmhouse. Betty Verga was the matriarch of the family operation.

"No, I usually smell the fresh peach blossoms and the sweet fragrance when I walk through the rows when I pitch in to help. This morning, I was walking through and noticed it was off. A sour sort of smell," Willie said.

Betty frowned. "That'd be canker."

Willie heard about bacterial canker from the other farmhands. They were talking about it while working one of the other orchards a year or two ago. "Want me to go tell Jack?"

"Know what, Willie? I trust you to run out there and check a few of the trees. See if any of them are dropping leaves or if you see the brown cankers on the limbs. If you do, mark them."

"I'll grab the purple ribbon."

"Make sure it stands out," she called as Willie trotted up the stairs toward the barn.

He used the jalopy to drive out to the area and parked along the dirt roadway. It wasn't an actual road, but one that had worn the grass from routine travel. The area he noticed earlier did have more leaves on the ground. Going up to one of the trees, he found cankers on the limbs. The fruit that came in had brown spots. Willie tied a ribbon around the base of the tree and checked over twenty more. He found thirteen with signs of infection. After seeing the speckled fruit, he was afraid it was worse than canker—it could be brown rot.

He noticed Jack was in the office when he headed out to the infected patch. With the ribbons tied, he glanced back, wondering how they were going to handle it, and if it was going to destroy the season's output. If it was brown rot, the trees' fruits would have spores. The surrounding trees could be infected with no signs. He hopped back in the jalopy and headed to the office.

Willie jumped out and ran up the steps. He paused to

knock on the door.

"Come in," Jack said.

Willie entered the farmhouse where Jack's office was situated in the front room.

"Hey, bud, what's up?"

"I think the southwest lot has canker, maybe brown rot. I marked the trees."

Jack pushed away from his desk and grabbed his baseball cap from the standby door. "You know what to look for?"

"Yes, sir. The bark on some of the limbs has cankers. Some are bleeding, none of them look sunken. But the fruit has brown spots," Willie reported. "They're all marked with purple ribbon. Do you want me to check other trees for signs?"

Jack looked out of the window at the hundreds of acres filled with fruit trees. Willie could see the concern form creases around the aged man's eyes. "No, first show me where you found them. I want to get a good look at the progression. I'm not gonna lie, Willie, I'd rather treat the Xanthomonas arboricola pv. pruni than deal with brown rot. Let's get going." He took a set of keys from the key rack on the wall and left the door open on his way out.

Willie was quick on his heels. "Should I go back to the market? I haven't been down there, only this morning to stock."

Jack climbed into his green Chevy pickup and waved to Willie to join him in the cab. "No, it's not busy yet. I need to see these trees and only you know where they are." He started the truck when Willie was seated beside him. "No matter what the cause, cankers are worrisome. We need to act quickly."

Willie nodded in agreement. "How do we treat it?"

"Well," Jack said. "It depends. If it's canker, we have to disinfect the equipment between trees. We cut the limbs back behind the cankers and burn the clippings. Everything comes from either fungus, bacteria, or pests. Each has its own solution. Unfortunately, I've seen it all."

After a few minutes, they arrived at the patch of trees Willie had marked. The bright purple ribbon stood out in the sea of greens, oranges, and pinks. Jack hopped out of the truck and waited for Willie to follow him.

"Yup," Jack said, stepping up to one. "That's the smell."

"So, it is canker?" Willie more confirmed than asked.

Jack examined one of the oozing spots on the limb and turned to look at Willie. "You sure were right. Come on, let's get back to the barn so I can gather the guys. We need as many hands on this as we can afford. You check in with Betty, then meet us here. I want you to learn how to stop this menace in its tracks."

The likelihood of the canker spreading made Willie even more aware of the fragility of the peach trees. He loved the fragrance, the fruit, and working at the orchard. And he was grateful for the opportunity to learn. He was curious about how to keep botanical diseases at bay. They were the cause of many orchards losing hundreds of trees and thousands of dollars' worth of product.

He knew that in the agricultural industry a downgrade in production could lead to an entire orchard folding. It may take years, but once the soil was tainted it had the potential to infect new saplings. Saplings were costly, as were the chemicals used to treat diseases and the process of combating them in an efficient manner.

After restocking the market with fresh pickings, Willie hopped into the jalopy with another worker. He helped Willie so that they could head to the group working on the diseased trees. Their job was to drive the clipped and pruned debris to a barren section of land. They would be able to burn them without risk of losing control of the fire, and without infecting any nearby trees with escaped spores.

When Willie arrived home, his mother had creamed tuna bubbling in a pot on the small white stove. Willie hurried upstairs to change and wash up for dinner. He still had night chores to do at home, but he didn't see them as daunting tasks when he knew the importance of being responsible. He and Eddie headed down to dinner and sat with his younger brothers. His father had just settled into his own chair.

"So, what's new today?" William Sr. asked no one in particular.

While waiting for his mother to finish the dish, he decided to tell his father about his findings. Being an airborne disease, he thought it could be a potential issue among some of the peach farmers in the co-op. "I spent the day pruning trees with canker."

"No kidding," William Sr. said, appearing more interested. "You know how to spot that?"

Willie nodded, eager to share his knowledge. "Yes, sir, I do. I'm the one who noticed the sour odor and talked to Mrs. Verga about it."

William Sr. sat up in his chair. "Oh, is that so?"

"I was thinking maybe we should tell Mr. Riley and Mr. Mortin. They have ten acres each filled with peach trees and it's airborne. Not saying they're going to have it, but better to check the trees than not, I would think."

"That's good thinking there, Willie." He sat back and crossed his ankle over his knee. "After dinner, I want you boys to go check ours and your grandparents' trees. They could get Cytospora canker which can be airborne too but sets in from water. Like pruning before a rain, the open wounds allow the spores to get in. Look for any oozing or yellow spots on the bark. We don't need to lose any trees over it."

Willie and his brothers took off to scour the orchard for any signs of rot or cankers or any other disease they could think of. They looked for anything out of the ordinary before heading back to the house. They were thankful not to find a thing. William Sr. sat on the porch step, waiting for the boys.

"I was thinking. Maybe you should go talk to Mr. Riley and Mr. Mortin on your own," he said.

"Really? Okay, Dad." It was rare for Willie to call his father Dad, but at the moment he thought it right.

"Absolutely," his father said, leaning back on his elbows that he had propped on the porch floor behind him. He was two steps down and the position put him at chest level with Willie. "You know what to look for and what to do about it. Perhaps they do, perhaps they don't. But experience always serves its purpose. You've proven to have that experience."

Willie sat on the lower step. "We have to keep watch for the next couple of years, Jack said."

"Oh, yeah? Why's that?"

"Because signs don't always show right away, and there could be something else underlying. We have to look for mummified fruit, too. It can carry the spores and if it's brown spot, it doesn't die in winter."

"Then you'll have to make sure you keep on top of our four farms. You've got an eagle eye, Willie. And that is going to serve you well someday."

***

The next morning was Willie's day off from Verga. He walked over to the Riley property just after the sun was up. His mother was cooking bacon, so Willie grabbed a piece on his way out the door. He was eager to get to the farms, hoping he wouldn't find any evidence of the disease. Though he was aware of the work in front of him if he spotted anything foul.

He reached the ranch house steps, opened the aluminum screen door, and knocked. Willie enjoyed listening to Mr. Riley tell stories on Sundays. He was a retired high school science teacher and part-time adjunct professor in Sacramento. The man always dressed in a suit on Sunday, and khaki slacks and a button-down short-sleeve shirt wherever else Willie caught a glimpse of the man. His hair had gone salt and pepper gray, but his stature was straight, tall, and slender. He had spectacles that often slid down his high bridge nose.

Mrs. Riley was a retired elementary school librarian and taught Sunday school. She always had a smile for the little ones on Sundays. Willie thought the kids liked her because they followed behind her, eager to see what they were going to learn. She liked to tell stories as part of her lessons, even to the adults and older kids who stuck around after the service.

Mr. Riley opened the door and peered down at Willie. "Well, good morning there, young man." Like most of the other people in Willie's community, these people were simple. They lived off the land to supplement their income. These were hard-working people who made no excuses. They just kept going forward, no matter what cards were dealt. This work ethic rubbed off on Willie.

"Good morning, sir," Willie said.

"Your father tells me there may be a menace in the air. Let me grab my hat and we can go have a look." The man left the main door open while he disappeared inside.

Willie waited on the step with his back half to the screen door. He learned from Eddie that it was rude to stare into people's houses, but it was also rude to turn your back to them. The best of both worlds put everyone at ease. He thought his brother's advice was silly at the time, but being an older teenage boy, he found himself practicing what his brother preached more times than he could have counted.

Mr. Riley came back with a gray fedora and a plastic sandwich baggie that he folded and put in his pocket before joining Willie on the step.

"You know what this is for?" he asked.

"Leaves that might be infected?" Willie responded. "My boss at Verga worked with a team when the soil needed testing and that's how they collected samples."

Mr. Riley smiled. "That's right. And if we do, I have a lab where I can find the exact culprit. It will make eradicating the issue before it gets too far into the season easier. We're already halfway into the growing season."

Willie agreed, "Yeah, but maybe there won't be anything to worry about. After we walk through your trees, I'm heading over to Mr. Mortin's."

"If you don't mind the company, I'd like to tag along."

"Sure," Willie was surprised that Mr. Riley would want to spend his free time looking for diseased trees.

The two headed up the small hill lined with peach trees. They walked along the rows. Willie scanned the limbs of each tree for anything suspicious. When he spotted something, he did a closer inspection, but he didn't smell anything sour, and he didn't spot any oozing.

"I don't see any cankers, Mr. Riley."

"Good to hear, Willie. But we still have the section of plum trees." The man led the way toward another section of trees closer to Mr. Mortin's property line. "I believe our two properties shared the orchard before our deeds drew the invisible line."

Willie started his inspection. The sun beat down overhead, and his throat was parched. Each tree had beautiful leaves and budding fruit. Mr. Riley stayed a single pace behind. They walked along five rows and still nothing.

"Looks like I lucked out, Willie. Thank you for the peace of mind," Mr. Riley said.

But Willie had stepped closer to the last three trees. "Um, Mr. Riley? I think you have a problem."

12
YELLOW POLKA DOTS

Mr. Mortin was sitting on the front porch when Willie and Mr. Riley arrived. He had a straw hat and a glass of iced tea, the ideal situation for the scorching summer heat. Although it was usual weather for Northern California, the first few weeks took some getting used to after the milder spring temperatures. Most of the older members of the co-op enjoyed sitting on their wooden porches in the early morning. They often sat for hours, enjoying the shade and views of the blossoming or fruit-bearing trees, depending on the season.

Willie waved his arm as he approached his neighbor. "Good morning, Mr. Mortin."

The older gentleman stood, setting his glass on the small, weathered table, leaving an instant wet ring from the condensation. He was similar to Mr. Riley in that he was a hard worker who didn't complain. He had a love of family, God, and country. "Why hello, young man. What brings you by?" His smile faded when he saw Mr. Riley following Willie. "Riley, what's this about?"

Mr. Riley removed his hat and swiped his wrist over his brow. "Well, it seems there's a bit of trouble with some of the trees on the orchards in the region. Willie here was kind enough to inform me and look over my property. I'd like to say he didn't find anything, but."

"And you're here because he found a problem with mine?" the older man said, the inflection of his voice returned to the original calm he exuded before spotting Riley.

"Just a few trees, Mr. Mortin," Willie said. "If you don't mind, I'd like to look over yours to make sure it's all good."

The older man stepped off the porch and joined Willie and Riley. "Well, tell me what we're lookin' for, and we can get to it." He led the way down the first row of trees. "If you see it, point it out."

Willie took the lead. He studied the bark and inspected the dark spots. "We're looking for yellow powdery spots or oozing cankers. If we find them, the only way to get rid of it is to cut the infected area from the trees. The pieces have to be burned so that the spores don't go airborne, but the saws need to get disinfected between each tree."

"You sure know your stuff, Collins," Mr. Mortin replied. "You're like your father. A smart, knowing man, keen on doing right by others. I admire that in a man."

"Thank you, sir," Willie said. He continued down the path of trees. "You know, some orchards have as many as a thousand trees per acre. Any idea how many you have here?"

Mr. Mortin pointed to the lot in front of Willie and then circled around to the back of his house. "Fifty over five acres. We have vegetables and livestock, so there aren't as many as your folks."

Willie was grateful for the smaller number of trees. He could walk the property, checking the trees a lot faster if he didn't have to wait for the other gentleman, but he knew the importance of showing respect. He would go at a pace that was good for them and found himself enjoying the stories they told about their own teenage years. Each had farming jobs and were glad Willie showed responsibility.

Mr. Mortin spoke up first. "I remember what it was like being young. Sharp eyes, a good strong mind. Riley, you trust his judgment?"

"I do," Riley said. "He spotted mine when I was ready to put this threat behind me. Willie knows his stuff, even at a young age. He's been working for Verga for years. I think he's a protégé."

"Well, Willie. Why don't you go on ahead? You can move twice as fast."

"Yes, sir," Willie said.

He took off up the hill, scanning the tree trunks, limbs, and leaves. He followed the lines until they ended at the stone walls. He ended with the ones that were abutted against Mr. Riley's infected plums. There was a small section that had bubbling bark and a few with yellow powdery spots.

"There is a section of about fifteen trees. I think we can stop the spread with clipping and burning, but the burning needs to be done away from the orchard because it can go airborne," Willie said.

"Then let me go back to the university to see if there is a way we can thwart this threat," said Mr. Riley. "The diagnosis will at least give us the bacterium."

Something Willie noticed on Mr. Mortin's property as opposed to Mr. Riley was the number of pheasants running around. There were birds digging in the old fruits and leaves at the base of the trees. "You don't think they're part of the problem, do you?" Willie asked. "If they touch the fruit or leaves of an infected tree and go on to another."

"You made a good observation, the pheasants could very well be carriers," Mr. Riley said. "I think it would be a good idea to try and keep them all confined. Not let them into the orchard areas."

"Sounds like I'm going to need a pen," Mr. Mortin added. "They won't like that."

Willie knew that Mr. Mortin had emphysema; he overheard his mother talking with his grandmother about it not long ago. "I'll help you. I can come over after school tomorrow. It shouldn't take too long, and then we can start on trimming the trees."

"Why thank you, Willie. You're a fine young man," Mr. Mortin said. But this was not unusual. Willie learned at a young age that neighbors help neighbors, a farming and ranching rule. Willie was special but was taught the same as many other farm boys and girls.

Willie hurried the birds toward the front yard near the house. There was already a chicken coop. He assessed the area and determined the spot next to it would do well to contain the pheasants. "How about over there for the new pen?"

"Works for me, Willie. I'll see you tomorrow; you better get home and get some shut eye." Mr. Mortin went back to his seat on the porch.

"Good night," Willie waived and called back to both gentlemen.

The next week, Willie learned how to maintain healthy trees through enriching the soil with potassium from Mr. Riley. He confirmed the fact with Jack at the orchard. There were ways to keep the trees free from disease and that meant being present in the moment. Taking care of the limbs, feeding the soil, and trimming so there was little to no overcrowding. He managed to get a decent sized pen built for Mr. Mortin in a matter of hours so that they could get down to the business of curing the disease.

The trees at Verga were doing well, and there were more signs of canker as the harvesting was underway. Willie was once again asked to work in the vegetable patch because the late summer harvest required knowledgeable pickers. There was a bounty of zucchini which needed to be picked. He pulled his shirt sleeves down, laughing to himself as he remembered the first time he went to pick summer squashes when he was thirteen.

He was appointed by Jack and soon learned that zucchini had little thorns on the stems. They were soft fine spurs and Willie didn't know to bring gloves or anything with him. The first day of zucchini harvesting he went home with bright red scratches up his arms. He wondered why the workers always wore long-sleeved shirts and soon discovered that he too would wear long sleeves to keep the thorns from scraping and cutting his skin. He understood that sometimes in life he had to learn things the hard way.

When he went home that evening, William Sr. was sitting at the table. He glanced up from his newspaper at Willie and looked at his red arms. "Son, what happened?"

"I was picking crookneck and zucchini squashes," Willie replied.

"Then I guess you'll wear long sleeves the next time."

Willie knew that his father did not accept complaining. As a Korean War veteran who was one of the highly decorated, famous *Frozen Chosin*, he would tell Willie and his brothers, *"Don't complain because nobody cares. Everyone has their own issues in life, and they are all worried about their own person."*

He grasped the first squash of the season and tossed it into his bucket, grateful for his father's words. Those were one of the many life lessons his father taught, and that stayed with him, even into his elder years. They were tidbits of wisdom, no matter the harsh undertone to the sound or the reminder that life was reality. You chose your journey and how you embarked on it. You and only you build your future no matter what is given to you in life. He also made sure Willie knew that it didn't mean people didn't help one another. He understood the balance of life. The one that meant you had to give to get; you had to build to achieve. Life would give you what you put into it. And the never give up attitude was the philosophy Willie carried through high school and later in his adult life.

13
THE CAMP

After an eventful school year, Willie had a busy summer before him. He was done working on the peach farm in the evenings, and because he was getting older, didn't have to formally check in with his mother anymore. He and his brothers still loved to wander around the house in their briefs and boxers while grabbing a plate of toast and eggs before getting ready and heading out for work on the farm every morning. Life was busy for the young country boys.

At church, the congregants held fellowship outings. These outings included summer camp—one for the boys and one for the girls. Then there were the camps for the teens, though they were still separated by gender. None of the Collins boys attended because they worked on the farm over the summer. Willie was still working at Verga Orchards, selling fruit and working in the fields. The camp lasted two weeks and was up in the Sierra Nevada mountains.

Not that Willie wanted to attend.

He liked working. It was a break from school and gave him interaction with people who stopped along the main road at the Verga farm market. He met people from all over the country and sometimes from abroad. More often than not, he met a lot of Bay area and Southern California customers on weekend road trips. So that meant that he had to be on the ball when droves of customers stopped in on a Saturday, and the peaches, pears, and plums would need constant replenishing.

Willie's apparel made customers laugh because he wore a white T-shirt that said, *Don't squeeze the peaches!* People had a tendency to look at the peaches, smell them, and give them a good squeeze. This would bruise the peaches and cause the areas that were touched to discolor and become unsellable. To avoid this, the Verga brothers came up with a plan to have Willie wear the shirt.

"Willie," Mr. Verga retorted. "How is the shirt working?"

"Not so good," Willie said. He turned back on his heels to face Mr. Verga. "For some reason, they see my shirt and just go on squeezing the peaches!"

"Hmm," Mr. Verga muttered and walked away.

***

That summer Willie met even more people who were traveling on their way to Lake Tahoe. The nice thing about working at the farm stand was that Willie enjoyed seeing the occasional beautiful young girls who stopped for fresh fruit on their way up to the mountains.

It seemed that the girls liked his long auburn hair and the curls that gathered behind his ears. There were times he tied a handkerchief around his head so he could keep his hair back while stocking. Running up and down the stairs to the basement store required him to keep the hair out of his eyes.

Seeing the girls heading to the mountains reminded Willie of the girls from church who were going to the girls' camp. Willie, Dwayne, and Spence decided to check out the teen girls' side. It was within driving distance, and they weren't under a curfew. At the end of the day, the boys called the girls and hatched a plan to sneak into the girls' camp.

Willie picked up the guys in the blue Chevy pickup at Spence's house and headed down the unlit, unpaved potholed road toward the hills.

"You sure you know where it is?" Dwayne asked.

"Yup," Willie assured.

Spence stuck his head out the window. "I don't see a camp anywhere. How far in are they?"

Willie shrugged. "We just have to head north."

"In the dark. It's nearly 10 o'clock," Dwayne said. "We're going to get shot for sure."

All three of them laughed, though Willie assured his friends. "We're not going to get shot. They don't have guns at girls' camp."

"There it is!" yelled Spence.

Willie pulled to the side of the dirt road and turned off the engine. He knew all the girls from his church, which made up about eight. They were expecting him. They made plans earlier in the week to meet up at girls' camp late at night. The girls would sneak out of their camp and open the locked gates to let the boys in.

"You come up and find us. We'll be in the cabin on the west side, closest to the gate," one of the girls said. "We'll hang a blanket out on the door."

"But be careful," another added. "There's security."

Willie remembered the phone conversation as he ran the plan through his head one more time.

Willie jumped out of the truck first. Dwayne and Spence were hot on his heels. They headed to the western side, which had a fence, but there was a point at the bottom that was weak. The three boys bent the wire, slid underneath, and headed to the gate the girls had unlocked. Sure enough, it was slightly ajar.

"Over here," Spence called. They crept around to find the girls' signal.

As planned, there was a handmade blue and white afghan hanging on a cabin door. Willie snuck up to it and knocked three times. He ran back around the side to his friends and waited for the girls to come out.

He watched the door as it creaked open.

"Psst," he said.

Five girls tiptoed to where he stood. They had their

hair tied back in ribbons and wore matching pajama sets. "Come on, you're gonna get caught," the girl in front exclaimed, waving her arms toward the boys.

They followed them inside the cedar-sided cabin. The girls' bunks had pink and red blankets with pillows on them. There was a small wood-burning stove in the middle. One of the girls had a frying pan on the top and was making grilled cheese sandwiches.

"You boys want some? We got the bread and cheese from the kitchen tonight."

"You bet," Spence replied before Willie and Dwayne could get a word out. "We're starving."

"Ahh, we'll take care of you," she said. "You guys are cute, coming all the way up here."

Willie and the guys ate the sandwiches while the girls told them stories about swimming in the lake and learning how to shoot a bow and arrow.

"I know how to shoot a bow and arrow," Willie said.

Dwayne confirmed, "We all do. We also need to know how to shoot a rifle because you never know when you have to defend yourself from a bear or wild animal."

"I never took you guys as the type to be worried about animals. There aren't any dangerous things this close to home," another said.

Willie laughed. "It's at least an hour from home, and there are only logging trails to get in and out. I wouldn't be surprised if you saw a cougar prowling around outside your cabin one night. They smell food and . . ." He swiped his finger across his neck.

The girls shivered. One slapped his arm. "Don't say things like that. The security guards can take care of anything if it comes along. But we're fine."

They continued to talk until each boy had eaten three sandwiches. The girls opened the door and stepped outside to make sure all the leaders and security guards were preoccupied. The one named Mary, waved for them to follow her.

Being the first out the door made her vulnerable. She was scanning the dark. Willie took advantage of her situation. "Reeeer," he hissed.

She squealed and ran back to the cabin. The other girls gathered her in. "Shh, you're going to get us all in trouble."

"Well, he scared me." She swatted at Willie's arm. Dwayne and Spence were laughing.

But they all stopped when they heard real rustling outside.

"You girls alright in there?" a male voice asked.

"Yes," Mary replied. "Just a bad dream."

"Okay, well, go back to sleep. We're here, so nothing to worry about."

"Thank you," she said.

They all waited until it was quiet again. "We have to get going," Dwayne urged. "They really will be on the lookout now."

"You worry too much," Willie said. He opened the door and poked his head out. "Coast is clear."

The three boys managed to get to the side of the cabin to hide in the shadows. "We'll stay here and go one by one," Spence said.

Willie agreed. "Sounds good to me."

"Me too," Dwayne said.

"I'll go first," Spence said. "I want to get out of here as fast as I can."

Willie and Dwayne nodded.

Spence crept to the edge of the cabin and looked out. "Clear." He crouched and ran toward the fence. But before he could reach the hole, a shot rang out. The security guard shot the dirt at Spence's feet.

"Stop right there, mister." Two guys grabbed Spence by the shirt and dragged him off toward the middle of the encampment.

All the girls started filing out of their cabins. The ones that Willie knew were waving him and Dwayne on. "Go!"

Willie and Dwayne didn't look back. They ran through the gate, slid on their bellies under the broken wire, and tore through the brush. They quickly arrived at the truck and sped off on the logging roads. Willie didn't use the main roads, and they didn't go back for Spence.

"Poor sap," Dwayne said, laughing.

"He almost got shot. Oh, man, that was close." Willie

eased off the gas and took the roads slower after a good five minutes. "I think we're in the clear, as long as Spence doesn't rat us out."

"Ah," Dwayne said. "He'd never do that. You never sell out one of your own."

"Yeah, well, we just left him there," Willie said through fits of laughter. "That might change things."

"Nah, we're tight."

***

Getting out of the camp without getting caught gave Willie and Dwayne the courage to go back a few more times while the girls were still up in the Sierra Nevada mountains at the girls' camp. Each time, the girls would make food and feed them. The boys ate fudge, pancakes, and marshmallow peanut butter sandwiches. It turned out to be one of the most exciting summer adventures of Willie's teenage life.

14

GIRLS

After the girls' camp raids and feasts, Willie became popular, not only with the church girls but also with his schoolmates and the cheerleaders. His reputation as an athlete didn't make him *the* most popular guy in the school, but he was close. He had girls passing him their phone numbers when they saw him in class the first week of school. There were love notes stuck in the vents of his locker, and others would giggle as they passed by him in the halls.

Back in eighth grade, Willie met his first girlfriend at the small county grammar school. There were no junior high schools in the small towns, only kindergarten through eighth grade. A girl named Linda. She had long, blonde hair and big, blue eyes. He asked her to be his girlfriend when she gave him a piece of her brownie during lunch after she saw him give his lunch to his friend. They dated, which meant hanging out during lunch, for two months before another boy caught her interest.

One day during recess, she approached Willie. "I'm sorry, Willie," she said, "but I've moved on. You should too."

Willie's eyes dropped down, looking at his feet. He wasn't heartbroken, but it stung. The first breakup. The next breakup wasn't until the following year in ninth grade when he sat next to a girl with dark brown hair. He was drawn to her light brown skin and pink freckles on her nose. Her name was Elizabeth. She was the one who broke his heart.

It was the week of midterms. Willie had gone to the library for resource material. He was looking up information about Thomas Jefferson for a paper. He went to the desk to take out a book about previous presidents when the girl who took his library card recognized him.

"Willie? What are you doing here?"

"Research. Got a paper due for Mr. Wendz."

"I have him too; he's tough. But I like the way he teaches history. I remember it so much better when he writes the timeline on the blackboard."

Willie did not agree. "I don't memorize well. But I like reading. I'm doing my report on Thomas Jefferson. How about you?"

"John Quincy Adams."

"Hey, you want to work on them together?" Willie asked. "I could meet you in the library during lunch."

She blushed, "Okay. See you tomorrow."

"It's a date," Willie said, winking at her.

The following day they met, and Willie's heart swooned. He was taken by her good looks, intellect, and wit. She used big words and knew her history down to the years, months, and days. He found himself lingering by the entrance of the school one day, waiting for her to walk in. When she didn't, his heart sank and he lost focus on the day. He went to talk with Dwayne who had been kept back and was now in the same grade as Willie. He'd missed too many school days and needed to recoup the lost time.

"I think I want to ask Elizabeth out," Willie said.

Dwayne nodded. "Do you like her?"

"Yeah."

"Then do it."

"But I'm not sure if she likes me."

"Willie, you'll never know if you don't take the risk. You say it all the time. You have to take risks to gain experience. Either she likes you or she doesn't."

"Right," Willie said. "If she doesn't, then I know that I have the courage to face a girl I like. If she does, then I gained a girlfriend who makes me smile."

"That's you, always looking up."

"Unless I'm skydiving, it's the only way to look. I learned from my Grandma Davis to just go forward. That is the only way to go."

Dwayne bumped Willie's arm. "That was lame, even for you."

"Hey."

Willie pushed him back. They kept pushing until

Willie looked up and saw Elizabeth. She walked into the lunchroom with her arm in a sling. He left the table and Dwayne to greet her.

"What happened?"

"I fell off my horse last night. My mom had to take me to the doctor. It's only sprained, they said. No break. But it hurts like crazy."

"I bet," Willie said. "Did you have lunch?"

"Yeah, my mom made sandwiches before we left."

"You can come sit with Dwayne and me, if you want." Willie was walking toward his table, just outside of the cafeteria in the open quad area, and realized Elizabeth was following him.

Dwayne got up. "Actually guys, I hate to run off on you like this, but I have to catch up with my guidance counselor before this lunch period ends."

Willie waited for Elizabeth to sit before taking his own seat. "Oh, hey. I wanted to ask you a question."

"What is it?" She blinked at Willie. Her long black lashes caught him off guard.

"I, uh." He glanced at the clock on the lunchroom wall. "Would you be my girlfriend?"

Elizabeth smiled. "Kind of corny and a little surprising, but, yes, I'd like that."

The two smiled at each other until the bell rang. "I'll see you by the front door of the school hallway tomorrow morning. No more falling off horses."

"Okay, and I promise I won't."

They went their separate ways and dated for the next four months. The relationship ended when neither one of them wanted it to. Elizabeth's father was in the Army, and she was moving to a base in Germany. They had no choice but to say goodbye. Willie's heartbreak didn't last too long. One of the girls on the cheer squad saw him doing push-ups for a test in gym class. Willie did the hundred and went on to sit-ups, then pull-ups. She was on track and was new to the school. He noticed her looking.

"Hi," she said, when he finished the calisthenics portion of class.

"Hi." He pulled the end of shirt up to blot his forehead. "You're the new girl on the cheer squad, aren't you?"

"Yup, Cassandra."

"Nice to meet you."

"You're ripped, huh?" Cassandra asked.

"Ripped," Willie exclaimed looking down a bit surprised. "Oh, I guess."

"I like that," she said.

"You wanna hang out sometime?"

It surprised him, but he missed being with a girl. He liked hanging out and chilling with girls. But he also liked being able to hold hands and share a sandwich or an extra cookie if he had one.

"Sure. We could run together after school if you

want?" Willie asked. He had basketball practice and worked at Verga Orchards after school a few days a week, but he always had time for a run. "See you later, then?"

"Yup."

She left, and their relationship lasted almost four months. Willie broke up with her because he met another girl who started up at the Verga farm market. She was helping him stock the fruit. He didn't feel a connection romantically with Cassandra, but he did still want to be friends.

"I like hanging out with you. Maybe we could stay friends?" he asked in a sheepish way, with his hands cupped together as if he were praying. "I think it's the same for you."

Cassandra agreed, "We get along, but it's not like a dating kind of like. Like, I like you, but not romantically. You're cute and all."

"Hey, no hard feelings. We're good friends. No reason not to stay that way." He meant well, but it was the dating that kept them meeting and running together. Once they decided to part, they didn't talk much. She had her running group and Willie went on to pursue another girl.

Each of the girls in Willie's life taught him something new about himself. He learned not to fear relationships because they may not last, but to embrace the time they shared together. He learned what girls liked, and he learned that they were all different. He hoped that they learned that he was a good guy and would always be there to lend a hand or talk. At the end of his school years, it would make him appeal to even more girls. And the more he worked, the more defined his muscles became. By junior year, Willie was maturing and getting noticed.

15
THE DANCE

P rom night arrived.

In the city schools, girls took to searching for the perfect dress in department stores while boys went suit shopping and then to the florist to order a corsage. Girls would get a boutonniere to pin on their man for the event and wisp their hair up in a mass of hairspray. Dark-framed glasses and bell bottoms with wing tip shoes were the social ideal. The guys picked up their girls in their cars and drove to the high school, which was decorated with streamers, ribbons, balloons, and flowers. A band would play on stage while the teacher and parent chaperones patrolled the grounds. It was a high time, filled with excitement and showing off.

The country prom was a different ordeal. It was less formal. Many of the boys and girls would settle for a more country look—cowboy boots instead of fancy shoes or a little country lace on the girls' dresses. When Willie put on his blue Sunday suit, he was dressed the same as any other week. The major difference was that he held a box with a homemade corsage his mother put together, and his wavy hair was combed back, the curls arranged around his ears and over the collar of his shirt. He was picking up Jill, the latest girl who caught his attention. She was blonde with hazel eyes and freckles across her nose, and she was one of the cheerleaders. Willie planned to pick her up in the blue pickup truck. Earlier in the day, he washed it off with a rag and bucket of soapy water. It was hard to make it look good with its old faded blue paint, but at least the dust was washed off, except for the dust that landed on it driving out of his dirt driveway and roads.

Normally, the seniors were the only ones to attend prom, but there were too few students graduating as the student body was minimal. The town only had a couple thousand residents and thought it best to have combined junior and senior prom. It doubled the attendance and allowed the seniors one more chance to show their moves and live out their dreams.

Dance shows like *American Bandstand* on television were popular, whether people lived in the country or the city. It was all the rage on Saturday mornings, and disco as a music form had taken the country by storm. Northern California was no exception. Though the girls wore dresses with a country flair that they ordered from the Spiegel or Sears and Roebuck catalogs.

Willie climbed into his truck and drove down the dirt road with their aging Irish setter chasing after him. More often than not, the dog would join him on walks or chase the vehicles that drove by. He watched her stop, panting in the road at the crest of the hill. Willie thought to himself, *It's as if she knew about Baxter's shooting habits too.* He laughed out loud. *He'd shoot at anything that didn't belong on his property.*

He pulled up to Jill's house, a small two-story farmhouse, much like his own. It was pale yellow with chickens and a turkey running around the front yard. They had a rabbit in a cage by the side of the house and three other cages that were empty. Willie's heart sank as he thought about the rabbit sandwiches he learned to eat out of kindness. He hoped Jill wasn't a fan of rabbit sandwiches.

Jill's mother appeared in the doorway. Her father stood outside with a pipe and denim jacket, waving for him to come over. Willie stepped from the truck and grabbed the wrist corsage for his date.

"You must be, Willie," her mother beamed. Her eyes sparkled, wet with tears. "Don't you look handsome."

Jill's father was sitting on the porch swing, a loaded shotgun leaned against the house nearby. He stepped down the porch stairs, hand outstretched. "I've heard good things about you. Like how you saved numerous crops over several seasons. That's life or death out here. You must be a fine young man."

Willie shook the man's hand. "Thank you, sir." In their small town, everybody knew everything about everyone.

"You coming straight home after the dance?" her father inquired.

"Yes, sir," Willie said.

"Then we'll see you at ten. It's Jill's curfew," her father added.

Willie nodded. "Yes, sir. But the dance ends at eleven tonight. Is it okay to come home right after that?"

"Okay, then, but don't be goofing around after," Jill's father exclaimed as he walked back up the creaky wooden steps to the porch swing.

Jill appeared in the doorway. It brought an instant smile to Willie's face. She stepped onto the porch and Willie beamed. She matched his color—soft blue. Her dress looped around her neck and gathered at the waist before hanging straight down past her knees. She had a pair of white gloves and a daisy pinned to her hair. But the new shiny cowgirl boots were the icing on the cake.

She waved at Willie.

Willie approached the steps and held out the corsage in front of him. His heart fluttered at the sight of her dressed in a simple ensemble that enhanced her natural beauty. He couldn't tell if she was wearing makeup or if her cheeks were blushing because of the occasion. Her lips shined in the evening sun, which hinted at her wearing some form of lipstick or gloss. "You look beautiful," he said.

"Oh, I need a picture," her mother said.

Jill stepped down to meet Willie, who towered over her small five-foot-five frame. Her mother snapped a picture with a small, black Kodak camera as Willie slid the corsage over her daughter's wrist. The tiny white flowers and single pink rose were enhanced with green leaves and wrapped with green tape; adorned with a white ribbon and a piece of lace from one of his mother's old dresses.

"Thank you, it's gorgeous," Jill said.

Willie escorted her to the truck, opened the door, and helped her into the cab. Once she was settled in the seat, he closed the door and ran around the truck bed, waving back at her parents.

"Be good and drive safely," her father called with a slightly scornful look on his face.

Willie stopped by his door. "I will, sir." He hopped in, turned over the engine, and eased out of their grass covered driveway onto the pothole filled dirt road. It was the road that led to the main route, which would take them to their destination.

"You clean up well," Jill said to him once they were driving.

Willie smiled. "Hey, I gotta work for a living. Besides, it wouldn't be a special occasion if I dressed like this all the time."

Jill laughed. "True. It would make people look. No one around here dresses like that. You'd be a spectacle."

"So what? You don't like a good spectacle?" Willie teased.

She blushed. "No, that's not what I'm saying, and you know it." She swatted his arm.

"Wait, are your cheeks getting red, Ms. Jill? I think you like the spectacle tonight."

"Okay, you need to stop. I'm done talking to you until you swear to behave. No more teasing."

Just as she said that they came into the clearing that opened into the town square. The majestic buildings of the bygone gold rush days were replaced with the upgraded town hall, a very small grocery store, the butcher shop, a feed store, and an auto mechanic garage. He wound up behind several other pickup trucks. Many of the pickup trucks had gun racks in the back windows with a rifle or two. Willie and Jill sat in line with their classmates heading to the same destination—the high school prom. It was Willie's junior year, but Jill was a senior. They started dating at the beginning of May, after she ran up to congratulate him for making the winning basketball shot to put the school in the playoffs.

The rectangular granite building was a mere six truck lengths ahead of them. Willie pulled into the parking lot and parked next to the grass. The doors to the lobby were propped open with a metal chair. Paper mâché bows of yellow, blue, and white hung over them. A hand-painted sign that read *Prom* hung down from the frame. Music streamed from the room. A guitar mingled with a male singer's voice. It was a popular love ballad of the time, Led Zeppelin's *Stairway to Heaven*. Though the singer was not quite good, he was okay enough for Willie to recognize the song.

Willie opened Jill's door and offered her his hand, assisting her from the seat. He was glad he took the time to wash the truck and clean off the old dusty bench seat. It was a consideration he hadn't forgotten—the dust from the farms and roads dirtying her dress. New dresses were one of the things he knew most folks in the area were unable to afford. He was well aware of the value and hard work that went into every penny. There were people in the town making less than a hundred dollars a week. When it came to purchasing unnecessary items, there were few families that had the ability. Jill slid out of the truck, pulling her skirt tight toward her shins to keep the fabric from touching the edges of the rusted vehicle's framework. The footboard was crumbling and could tear her dress, Willie was late to realize. He pulled her toward him.

"Don't want that to catch," he said, thinking he was smooth.

"Yeah, okay." Jill put her hand on his arm. "Thanks."

"Shall we?" he asked, arm poised to escort her to the source of the music.

They reached the doors where several teachers waited

to let them in. Each student had written their name on a pad to enter a raffle for an end-of-the-evening surprise gift. Willie wrote his name and handed the pen to Jill.

"I can't believe this is my last dance," Jill said as they stepped into the dimly lit gymnasium. "I'm graduating. It's unreal."

"I can't believe I will graduate next year. I know what you mean. It seems like time stood still but didn't all the same." Willie led Jill to a table with their friends.

"Looking good, Willie," Dharma said. She was sitting beside two empty chairs. Her own dress fell just below the knee and was a simple pink frock that she paired with a white knitted shawl. "You too, Jill. Come sit."

Willie pulled out a chair for Jill and straddled the chair beside her. "Pretty good turnout. Too bad Spence and Dwayne aren't here."

"Oh, Dwayne's here," Dharma corrected. "He went to go talk to some of the single girls."

"What about you?" Willie asked. "You're single."

"I'm good sitting right here. Why don't you ask Jill to dance? You didn't get dressed up to sit here all night, did ya?"

Willie looked at Jill and raised his brow. "Wanna dance?"

Jill shrugged and laughed. "I guess. What do you think? I've been waiting to dance."

He took her hand and made his way to the dance

floor. There was plenty of room because the gymnasium could hold over a hundred students and there were half that, though the night was still young.

Jill put her hands on Willie's shoulders. He put his hands high on her waist and began the slow, circular movement to the music. When the song ended, he watched the teacher grab a 45 record from a stack on the table beside it. The hi-fi system was a huge improvement over the last dance he attended where they used 45s to play on an old record player with big, dusty speakers.

He was twelve years old then, and it was the eighth-grade dance at the grammar school. The building hosted grades kindergarten through eighth grade, with the culmination of the final year before high school ending in the formal dance. Willie wore a Sunday suit that year. His mother dropped him off in the 1968 green Dodge Coronado station wagon. When he went inside the room, where he ate lunch every day, it was transformed into a crepe paper paradise. There were tissue paper flowers and paper mâché decorations on the walls. Streamers hung from the ceiling and on the retracted basketball hoops. The school was so small the gymnasium and cafeteria were the same room. There weren't a lot of kids at the time, with the town population being under a thousand.

There was a small cream-colored record player, with two speakers on the sides, situated on a desk. Earlier in the week, announcements were sent home asking for the students to bring records with them to provide music. He remembered that about sixty kids showed up for the dance that night, but only three brought records. One kid brought two 45 records and the other two brought three 45s each. One of the kids brought *I'm a Believer* by the Monkees, which was played twelve times. There were maybe ten other songs that played for over two hours.

Willie laughed out loud.

"What's so funny?" Jill asked.

He shook his head. "Nothing. I guess dances have come a long way in the last four years."

Jill nodded. Willie guessed she understood. They attended the same grammar school and had been a year apart all through their schooling. If he endured the cream-colored record player, then she had to have had the same one because he thought it was old at his eighth-grade dance. And if it worked in the country, it was a keeper. If it didn't work, it was kept anyway.

But this was country life; a good life that was like bliss. Everyone was poor, so the kids didn't know any better. Money really didn't matter and there was no keeping up with the Joneses. Instead, everyone helped each other out. The kids all seemed the same, not caring about big city luxuries. Hard working, country loving, God-fearing people lived there, and the kids were raised that way. Though there were differences and a few bloody noses here and there, everyone was close to being on the same page. How many songs played at the dance didn't matter.

After the last prom song ended, Willie and Jill, Dharma and Dwayne, and the rest of the kids wandered out into the parking lot. The end of the school year was upon them, which meant going to the local junior college or working full-time at whatever jobs they could get. Willie felt lucky to have kept his job with Verga Orchards throughout his teenage years, but he always knew he needed something more. He dropped Jill off at her parents' house, where they were sitting on the porch sipping sweet tea.

Willie hopped out of the truck, walked around the front, and opened Jill's door. She stepped down with less caution and more exhaustion. Most of the kids their ages had jobs and school during the year. Jill was no exception. She smiled at Willie, who walked beside her to the bottom step.

"Thank you, Willie. I had fun." She leaned over and kissed him on the left cheek.

"No problem. I had fun too. See you next week." He waved at her parents and went back to the truck. A mix of sixties and now seventies music replayed through his mind. He started the engine and eased onto the road, humming to the Monkees.

16
ALL WORK NO PLAY

The school year had ended. June 1 was around the corner. As far as Willie was concerned, it was the start of his senior year. He was chosen to play summer league basketball, but he had other obligations. There were costs involved in owning an old pickup truck, living in the country, saving for college, and a church mission. Gas prices were on the rise and insurance was his responsibility since Eddie bought his own car and had to make payments along with his own insurance bill. It was one of William Sr.'s teachings in the realm of responsibility, money management, hard work, and independence.

Willie never batted an eye at the thought of getting a job to help out the household financially or for taking on his fair share of the home expenses. He often took on extra responsibilities that included checking in on church members and running errands or completing odd jobs for his neighbors. He struggled with knowing he would have to give up the free time he did have if he got another job, but he would find a way. There were no such things as problems, only challenges. Getting a second job would present a new set of criteria to put some new solutions into play.

One day while stocking the farm market basement with peaches, eggplants, zucchini, and other produce at Verga Orchards, the older women were talking amongst themselves. Willie overheard Mrs. Verga discussing the meat market needing some help in the butcher shop. One of the kids that was helping out had left on a whim.

"He told Mitchell that he was leaving for Philadelphia with a group of his friends," Mrs. Verga said.

"What on earth for?" asked Agnes, one of the other ladies Willie had worked with over the last several years. "These young kids don't think of anything but what they want in the moment. Did he give poor Mitch any notice?"

Mrs. Verga shook her head. "None. Not even two weeks. I guess they have a band and want to try to hit it big and chase their dream. I don't know why they didn't start in Los Angeles."

"Now that would make sense. All the big record labels are right here in California. What's in Pennsylvania?" Agnes huffed. "I don't get all these dreamers. Backpacking across Europe, hitchhiking around the country, and just wandering aimlessly. It's a different generation, that's for sure. No mind for responsibility."

"Well, I wish them well," chimed in the third woman working the cash register. "If they have big dreams, I hope they get to glimpse a piece of their dream as part of their reality. I've been happy working on the farm for fifty-five years, though I had a different dream. I wanted to be an actress and got cast in a toothpaste commercial in the early sixties. Let me tell you, it made me realize how hard it is to break into the business, and that small part was gold. I'll never forget the experience, and I'm grateful to have had it. But it was no life for someone who wanted to raise a family and live in the beautiful country—country life is hard work and responsibility, but is bliss."

"Excuse me," Willie said. "Does the butcher shop still need help?"

"As far as I know," Mrs. Verga said.

"I'm looking to take on another job. If it's alright with you, I'd like to go talk to Mr. Cline about the position. I can run out there on my break."

"Tell you what, Willie," Mrs. Verga said. "You finish stocking here and head on over. Mitch was left high and dry. I'll ring him on the telephone and let him know I'm sending you over."

"Thank you, ma'am," Willie said. He hurried through the stocking and took the tractor back to the barn. There weren't any new crates to be put on the trailer yet, and the migrant workers were up for the season, so he knew there were enough hands to pick, load, and stock if he wasn't back before the afternoon rush.

One thing he learned by working in the fields and the farm market was that around two-thirty in the afternoon, when the kids were getting out of school, the Verga fruit market was flooded with people. He thought it might be because they needed food for dinner, the afternoon snacks, or for the next day's breakfast and lunch. Whatever the reason, Willie was grateful to have the job and to be employed at one of the busiest stands east of Sacramento.

Willie stopped in the office on the first floor of the house next to the barn. "Mrs. Verga, I finished stocking."

He saw her sitting behind the big desk in the back. She raised her finger to tell him to hold on a second while she was on the phone. Willie stepped inside and closed the door behind him. He tucked his hands in his pockets while he waited for her to finish.

"Yes, he is. The finest I've got. You won't be disappointed with him, Mitch," she said. "But remember, you only get him when he's not busy with us. In fact, he's standing right here. I'll go ahead and tell him." She listened and winked at Willie. "Alright, will do. Have a blessed day." She hung up and waved Willie over. "That was Mitch at the meat market. He's desperate for help because one of his guys called in so he's down two bodies. That's a lot in a service business. So, with that news, I'm thrilled to be the one to tell you . . . you've got the job. And remember, your main priority is here at the fruit market. We all help each other out in our small town. So, have fun cutting meat."

Willie couldn't contain the smile that spread across his face. All his hard work paid off. He had earned a reputation for his character. It filled him with pride, but he also felt humbled because he knew farm work—and loved it—but he didn't know the first thing about formal butchering. He saw it as an opportunity to grow; to move into a new phase of his life, one that involved taking risks and learning how to navigate the unknown.

"That's awesome," he said. "When should I go?"

"Right now. I made arrangements. We'll get by without you for today. You just get on over there. We'll see you back here for your normal shift tomorrow. Mitch will let you know when he needs you."

Willie left the office with a spring in his step. He climbed into his pickup truck and headed into the small town just a few miles away from the fruit market at Verga Orchards. He turned up the radio and listened to a static-filled song by the Mamas and the Papas, elbow propped on the window frame, and the wind blowing his hair. The sweat from the early morning heat dried on his skin as the air rushed through the truck. Working in the country made him feel alive. Going into town meant he was going to have a very different job. When he pulled into the dirt parking lot on the side of the white bricked building, he drove around back to where the employees' cars, trucks, and jeeps were parked.

He ran a brush through his hair and pulled on his long

sleeve button-up shirt that he wore for the morning work at the orchard. He always found the morning chill vanished once he started work, so he would usually take it off and head into the farm market in a T-shirt. Since he hadn't done any big jobs, the shirt he was wearing was still relatively clean. He fastened the buttons before going inside.

There was a glass door with a metal pull handle in the front with various old advertisements on the glass, including cigarettes and beer. A stand filled with newspapers and sales flyers sat by the front entrance. Shopping carts were lined against the building, and a soda machine stood like a majestic red beacon among them. The butcher shop was in the back of the little grocery market. The market could not have been more than two thousand square feet.

Willie went inside and headed to the little office at the end of the cash register row. He knew Mitchell Cline from errands he ran for people in the church. They often had requests for specific cuts of meat, and Willie was the one to ensure they got their packages.

"May I help you?" asked a young woman Willie thought to be in her twenties. She had dark brown hair that hung straight to the middle of her back; the bangs were secured above her ears with two metal barrettes. Her short sleeve brown shirt had blue flowers and complimented her orange pedal pushers. She was wearing a store apron.

Willie stepped up to the counter. "I'm here to see Mr. Cline about a job in the butcher shop."

"Oh, let me get him. By the way, I'm Liz."

Liz turned her head back and yelled, "Someone here to see ya, Cline!" She turned back and gave Willie a smile. She had beautiful, piercing light blue eyes. "He'll be here in a second," she said.

It didn't take long for the five-foot, ten-inch man to make his way to the front. He sported a long white apron covered with red blood and a white ball cap. He had a knife holder on his hip, like a Western gunslinger—but instead of guns, it was filled with knives. "You must be Willie Collins, the Verga boy, I think. I've seen you around here on occasion."

"I do errands for folks that need help," Willie offered. "They can't always get to the store."

Mitch clasped Willie's shoulder. "That's mighty fine of you, young man. There aren't many who take others' needs into their own hands."

Willie nodded. "Yes, sir. I was telling Mrs. Verga I wanted another job after I learned that you had a position open." Willie paused and stared him in the eyes and exclaimed, "I'm a fast learner!"

"So, I've been told. Follow me," he said, heading to the back of the store from where he came. "You ever do any butchering?"

"No, sir."

"Well, I guess that's good, because I can teach you the way I do things. It's harder to break old habits than to teach new techniques."

They walked into the back room, which was cold. There were metal counters and sinks with knives and wooden boards. Willie spotted a cleaver beside a large chunk of red meat that he guessed was beef. Out of the corner of his eye, Willie saw a small mouse scamper in the back corner and go between the crack of a wood floorboard. The old wood floor was covered in sawdust. It was a little slippery, but Willie quickly figured out that it was soaking up spills and blood.

"Okay, Willie," Mitchell said. "The purpose of a butcher shop is to offer various cuts of meat to customers. The shop has a display case showing different cuts, such as steaks, roasts, pork loin chops, and ground beef. Customers can interact with the butcher, who can assist them in selecting the desired cuts and quantities of meat. The shop would be equipped with meat processing equipment, including knives, saws, and grinders, to prepare the beef according to customer preferences. Now, I know you don't have the skills to do all these things yet, but I'm going to start you off on the most popular cuts."

"What is that?" Willie asked, pointing to an old wooden barrel sitting in a corner filled with a murky liquid.

"Oh," said Mr. Cline. "That's just the corned beef sitting in the brine."

"Wow, that really smells!" exclaimed Willie.

"Yep," muttered Mr. Cline.

Willie nodded to show he was on board for whatever Mr. Cline wanted him to do. The experience was new and exciting. He followed the man to a large sink, where they washed their hands before heading to a butcher-block table.

"Okay, Willie. I'm going to do the first one and then hand it over to you. This is sirloin, or sirloin tip. I'm going to cut this into sirloin tip steaks. After that, we take the top round and cut that into London broil steaks."

"Is this a whole side of beef?" Willie asked. He saw the different lumps of fat-trimmed beef muscle, and it was a bit small for the size of the animal he knew it came from.

"No, it's a quarter of beef," Mr. Cline affirmed. "Now, once you are done with these, I'll have a few more. I'll show you how to tie up the eye round roast and then we'll wrap them in butcher paper."

Cline pulled a long, slender knife from his leather tool belt. He pulled the sirloin tip toward him and began skimming the thick white covering that Willie recognized was fat. "This thinner, more see-through stuff is fascia. It makes the meat tough. We want to skim all this off to get down to the red muscle." Once he turned the piece over several times, ensuring the meat was trimmed, he slid the knife through the piece with ease. "This is how you cut the steaks. It's the same with the London broils, just performed on a different section of muscle. I'll show you the breakdown in about a week. This way you can get the hang of making straight cuts. Remember though, safety first. Let me go through a few safety rules." Mr. Cline began to teach Willie some safety rules when using a knife. That's when Willie noticed another younger, handsome butcher in the corner with dark black hair and blue eyes. He was working fast at cutting meat.

Willie watched and eventually took over. He made quick precise cuts that resulted in even slices. He piled the steaks on the side. Before the day's end, he had tied ten eye rounds, cut countless sirloin steaks, and almost thirty London broils. A week later, Willie was working on different meats. He worked with chicken, duck, beef, and pork. The loin chops were the most popular cut of pork. When he asked what made it so highly sought after, Mr. Cline told him that it was from the area closer to the spine. Customers who visited the shop requested loin, which they prepared and packaged as needed.

Mr. Cline wrote *Loin Chops* in black marker on the butcher paper. "These are known for their tenderness and flavor, Willie." He handed it to the elderly lady waiting at the counter.

Later, he learned that these were taken from the same section as the NY strip, another popular cut. But the pork loin chops were the most popular pork cut that many customers came to the shop to order.

That summer and early autumn, Willie worked seven days a week. He would go to the orchard on weekdays, starting at six in the morning and working until about three in the afternoon, unless they needed him to help with picking. Then he would drive over to the meat market. After the peach, pear, and plum seasons were over, he shifted his schedule to mainly butchering with Mr. Cline. He moved on to cutting up butchered pigs and learned that no matter the animal; the loin was a hot commodity. But the loin chops from the farm-grown slaughtered pigs didn't stay in the case.

He found himself filling orders for custom cuts on slaughtered pigs. Because he felt that the loin was regal and to give a twist of humor to the job, Willie took to marking all the highly regarded cuts as *Lion Chops*. The inside joke was enjoyed by all the customers and earned him a chuckle from Mr. Cline, though he requested that Willie spell it correctly on the customer packages. It was a learning experience that he would look back on and realize that each job he took showed him who and what he wanted to be.

He was a country boy and loved working on the farm and at the butcher's shop. However, the butchering life wasn't for Willie. He worked for Mr. Cline until the school year was underway, and then left with ample notice and on good parting terms once Mr. Cline was able to hire other butchers. Willie was not needed, and he could focus all his attention on school, the farm, girls, and sports.

17
NO MORE SHOTS

Willie's family farm sat on a hill with sloping pastures. The large farm to the west was sprinkled with cattle grazing in open fields and had a small, year-round creek. It was idyllic and beautiful. It was flanked by an old single-wide trailer on top of the hill with a beat-up broken-down shack that was used as a barn. This was old man Baxter's place. He was a decorated Vietnam War veteran with some war issues still lingering. Willie was shot at, along with Dwayne, Spence, Eddie, and even Maisy, the family's Irish setter. Mr. Baxter shot at any beast or person who dared venture too close for his comfort. But it had been more than a year since Willie had heard any shots when walking through the ranch to some of the fellas' houses.

Being bogged down with work from one school season to the next, he wasn't around to go hiking or to take romps through the pastures like he used to when he was younger. Nor was he around to hear if Baxter was still shooting at kids who stopped in the road next to his front yard.

Willie always admired Baxter's lawn; it was actually

a pasture where the cows came up to the trailer while grazing because the grass was bright and vibrant from the sprinkler he used to keep the beating sun at bay. Willie likened it to the irrigation system at the orchards. Even the people in his co-op used sprinkler systems or irrigation systems to keep their trees producing. It was another reason to keep the number of trees to a minimum of fifteen feet apart. The fruits came in healthy when the land was not overpopulated with flora. However, the best system was a basin where dams kept the water, and the root systems would collect it from the drainage rather than from the surface level where the possibility of evaporation beating absorption was high.

Baxter's system always went on in the evening, and before the sun came up. Willie assumed it was on a timer, but he wasn't sure, as he often saw old man Baxter walking the pasture, changing the irrigation pipe sprinklers.

One Sunday morning, on Willie's day off, he made plans to meet with Dwayne after church. They decided to meet at the stone wall at the edge of the road, off Willie's grandparents' property. It was at the crest of the hill and offered a beautiful view of the sunlit fields.

"Hey, stranger," Dwayne said as Willie made his way through the trees.

Willie smiled with the warmth of old friendship. He missed the days spent with Dwayne, full of laughs and adventures. Responsibility took precedence, and now the two friends had to schedule times to meet or seize moments when they came. Dwayne had two jobs and used the money to pay bills. His mother was barely able to make ends meet ever since her husband passed away from cancer. "How's your mom?"

"She's doing okay. Taking on laundry orders for people to fill the gap on Sunday. You know how everything is closed today. The extra few dollars can stretch. How's your fam?"

"Good." Willie kicked at a small rock and sent it flying across the road into a tree. "Think Baxter's watching us?"

"When doesn't he keep watch? You know, he inherited that trailer from his folks after they passed. The ranch has to be at least a hundred acres, but you never see him out there doin' much, other than changing the irrigation," Dwayne said.

"After fighting in Vietnam, I think he is probably done with being outside."

The boys studied the trailer windows. Willie's heart always raced when he was near the place. The first time he was shot at created a level of anxiety that could only be felt when he was near that property.

Dwayne poked Willie's arm. "Want to race to the back of his barn?"

"And chance death before graduation?"

"Chicken in your old age?" Dwayne teased, raising his

eyebrow and sticking a long stalk of oats in his mouth.

Willie smirked. "Fine. Last one there's a dead man."

The two boys took off running along the stone wall to where Willie's property opened to Baxter's. They leapt over the gate and ran neck and neck toward the big red barn. The cows were further down the pasture, so Willie felt safe running through the waist high grasses. He pulled ahead of Dwayne, but the boy grabbed for his arm, making him stumble.

Dwayne took the lead.

Willie ducked into the high weeds; afraid his laughter would be heard. "Your cheating's going to get us shot."

"Maybe," Dwayne laughed, "but I'll still win."

"With a bullet in your leg," Willie huffed. He pushed back to his feet and bolted after his friend. He caught up to him in time for the old man's dogs to start barking. Willie and Dwayne darted behind the barn.

No shots were fired.

"I guess we lucked out," Willie said. "Maybe he's asleep."

"Or out," Dwayne offered.

"Did Baxter ever go out? Guess I never thought about it, but he had to get food from somewhere. Only thing to buy today is gas."

Dwayne squinted at the house from the corner of the barn. "Maybe."

They stayed there, staring at the windows. Willie

thought he saw movement in one of the blinds and there was a light on in the end room. "He's waiting for us to come out. I just know it."

"Then we sit here a little longer." They stayed, watching for close to an hour. They could see what looked like movement in the trailer but were not sure.

"I think we can head back. He hasn't come out," Dwayne said.

Willie nodded. "On three."

"One," Dwayne said in a whisper.

"Two," Willie replied.

"Three!" they said together.

Willie burst from behind the barn at a full run. Dwayne appeared at his side. The cows had gotten closer but still weren't close enough to reach them. Willie glanced back over his shoulder every few seconds, trying to see if the back door was open or if Baxter had his twenty-two rifle raised.

They reached the opening and leapt over the gate, collapsing to the ground to catch their breath. Willie laid back on the grass, his hand on his stomach. "That was awesome."

"But weird," Dwayne reminded. "He always comes out. Even if he can't see what's there, he comes out just because of the dogs."

"You don't think something happened to him, do you?" Willie said through panting breaths.

"Nah, he's Baxter. He's tough. He'll live forever!"

"I say we return tomorrow night. I'll bring Maisy and you bring your dog, Dutch," Willie suggested. "We'll have them to distract his dogs so we can hide in the barn."

"Yeah, let's do that," Dwayne agreed.

***

The following evening after dinner, Willie headed up to the gate. He and Dwayne planned to meet there instead of the roadway because of their intended stake out. Maisy happily followed Willie, her tail wagging as she ran laps around him. When he got there, he had to wait for Dwayne. He knew that his friend's mother worked late and Dwayne would have to take care of the evening chores on their small farm. The usual routine was putting the chickens in their coop for the evening so that the wild animals didn't get them. Foxes loved them and often raided the locals' chicken enclosures. There was also a cow that Dwayne had to feed and secure in the barn, and a goat to put with her. They inherited the goat from his grandparents and used it for milk. When she had enough milk, Dwayne's mother would make goat cheese and they would eat that instead of meat when they ran low on eggs. The number of chickens they owned doubled since Willie's family moved up to the farm.

Dutch came running along the wall on Baxter's side and leapt toward Maisy, who was racing around the plum trees. The old man's dogs started howling. "Maybe bringing the dogs wasn't such a good idea," Dwayne said. "They make more noise than the trains."

"Maybe, but I don't see any movement and he hasn't come out yet."

"Don't count our chickens before they hatch," Dwayne said. "We don't want to get the dogs shot." As he spoke, Maisy led Dutch through the broken wood on the gate and off through the pasture.

Baxter's dogs barked at the door; ferocious growling filled the evening's quiet. Regardless, Willie and Dwayne crept through the overgrowth in the pasture. "I don't care what they do, we need to keep low. He might think it's just a wild animal if he can't see us," Willie said.

Dwayne gave him a thumbs up and took turns leading the way to the barn. Maisy and Dutch circled back and were staying closer to the guys. When they reached the barn, Willie signaled to Dwayne and whispered, "Let's go inside. We can see more and hide in the stalls."

"Agreed. Maybe those two will settle down. They're going to give away our position."

"Dwayne, I think that's a given. If Baxter is home, then he's watching and already knows our whereabouts. Don't you think it's strange we haven't seen him, and he hasn't even opened the door?"

"Let's stake it out and see what happens. He's a loner, Willie. Just because we haven't seen him doesn't mean he's not alive."

"If he's there, we're sure to be shot."

Willie shrugged, then climbed into a stall, tucking behind a stack of hay. The cows were down at the other end of the pasture and never saw the boys. They stayed there for over two hours. It was nearly full dark, and still no Baxter. Willie stood to brush the hay from his clothes. "Something's not right, Dwayne. We should have seen him by now. It's weird."

One of the cows had come up the field, causing Dutch to take off after her—Maisy followed. "I'm not chancing anything," Dwayne said and took off running toward the stonewall and the safety of the gate.

"Wait up!" Willie called, catching up to his friend, waiting to hear the crack of Baxter's shot.

18
COURAGE

The crack of the rifle never came.

Willie and Dwayne sat in Willie's pickup truck. "Thanks for giving me a ride," Dwayne said.

"No problem. What do we do about Baxter?" Willie asked. "I'm not sure we should sneak up to the house or anything, but I can't help feeling something's wrong." He drove past the trailer, slowing to a crawl.

Dwayne pointed. "He has to be in there. The lights are on, the sprinkler goes on every day, and the dogs are fine."

"How about I stop, and you go knock on the front door? He's less likely to shoot if you come from the road instead of the back of the property," Willie assured. "Besides, I can keep her running, so all you have to do is knock and run back. I can take off faster than he can get the gun out the door."

"Are you out of your mind? I'm not going up there. You go."

"I can't go," Willie reasoned. "I've got to keep the truck running for the getaway."

"Well, I'm not going up there alone. Heck, I don't want to go up there at all."

Willie frowned at Dwayne who shrugged. "I know he'll shoot. Call me a coward, but I'm not stupid. I'm staying safe on the road behind this hunk of metal." Willie patted the roof of the truck's cab.

"What if we just peek in the windows? We can duck down beneath the trim. We just have to be real quiet to keep the dogs from going off. They're like a bunch of sirens. Every time they hear something, they're howling and carrying on," Dwayne said.

"I don't know, Dwayne. Let's just call it a night and keep an eye on the place. We don't want to get killed for checking in."

"You got that right. Let's go, Willie. My mom's gonna be home when I get there. The last thing I need is a gunshot wound."

Willie drove to Dwayne's house. He backed into the dirt patch that was his friend's driveway, Dwayne jumped out, and Willie drove home. But when he got to the top of the hill, he stopped outside of Baxter's place. He contemplated going on his own but thought better of trespassing in the night. *It would probably give the old man a fright, or worse,* Willie thought. *He might think I'm some kind of animal trying to get inside.*

The rest of the week, Willie drove to school, taking notice of all the signs of life in the trailer. The dogs were still barking; the sprinkler was going, and the lights were on. He thought he saw movement behind the curtain at the front window so he sped off. That was proof enough to keep him from slowing down and checking in for a good week.

Being Willie's last year of high school, he became preoccupied with academic obligations. There was a history paper due, and research had to be done at the town library. The school library didn't have a big enough selection of resources, but the one in town could order what he needed from the city library. He had algebra homework that took him several hours to do, but English proved to be easy for him and something he really enjoyed. In fact, Willie loved writing and creating more than anything. Maybe he would even write a novel someday.

The teacher assigned short stories and Shakespearean plays that reflected on change. His teacher told the class that literature was a gateway—a direct link between the past and present. She talked about the importance of language, historical accuracy, and the need for more libraries because illiteracy was a big problem in our country. Willie found the short stories to be easier to understand and more interesting than the Shakespearean plays.

"Shakespeare was an artist," his teacher said.

"He created his own words. Why can't I create mine?" one of Willie's classmates responded. The students laughed, causing the teacher to smirk at them.

Willie hadn't actually seen his teacher get angry with any student, even after a smart aleck comment like that one. Although he agreed that Shakespeare was difficult, he respected the teacher and her opinion. He did, however, join the class in laughter. It was winter and the clouds had rolled in, and the mood as a whole was glum.

"Alright, glad you all had a good laugh. Now, back to the lesson. Graduation isn't for another five months, and you all have to pass this class if you want to walk across that stage," she warned.

"But it's boring," that same student said.

"Boring or not, you need to know this stuff because it's going to be on your exams. I don't control what the state expects of its students. Now, open your books to *The Merchant of Venice*. I want you to read the first act over the weekend and write a brief summary for each character in the play. You can't use the character list because you haven't been introduced to them all yet, but you can skim through and write down all the names you see before reading and taking notes."

Willie rested his head on his palm. He was grateful he gave up the meat market position and only worked at the orchard as needed in the off season because he knew this assignment alone was going to take time. He didn't have to go anywhere on Sunday after church, but he did have to do the chores around both his and his grandparents' properties. Not to mention anything he had to do to help out the church members who depended on him to run their weekend errands.

"You with us, Willie?" the teacher asked.

"Just thinking about fitting in the homework," he said.

She pursed her lips before she spoke. A gesture Willie had determined meant that she was undecided about the validity of the situation or comment. "It's not a long one. It should only take an hour at best for the writing. Maybe two if you read and go back through. Besides, you have all this evening and the next two days."

He nodded to let her know he understood. Willie was never the kind of student to complain. Instead, he did what he needed to get the best grades he could. Though not an A student, he worked hard to get B's and C's. It was his way. He was seasoned with his method and knew that he would be sitting up well into the night for at least part of the weekend. He just didn't fully grasp the content or even completely understand how to convey his own thoughts, but Willie was good with words and storytelling. His English grades helped bring up his poor grades in math and science, and it would all be well.

Dharma met Willie in the hall by the lunchroom. "Dwayne's waiting for us inside."

"I've got tuna on white bread," Willie said. "How about you?"

"Peanut butter and jelly, like always," she said.

Willie led the way to where Dwayne sat. He was drinking a carton of milk and had his sandwich wrapped in tinfoil on the table. "What took you slow pokes so long? I'm starving?"

"I had English. We're starting Shakespeare," Willie said.

"Oh, I love Shakespeare," Dharma interrupted. "But I can't understand it like I should."

"That makes two of us," Dwayne said.

Willie sighed. "At least you like it. I endure the material. Let's leave it at that."

Dwayne laughed. "I take it no Baxter watching then?"

Willie unwrapped his tuna sandwich and took a bite. "Not this weekend. I'll be elbows deep in homework. Maybe you can go knock on his door, finally. If you have the courage."

Dwayne shook his head. "Nope. Not touching it. That man will shoot me faster than you can say dead. Especially because I'm not his neighbor. At least he sees you and knows your cars. You've got that pickup truck and now you have that yellow Land Rover you just bought."

"You got a Land Rover, Willie?" Dharma asked. The excitement in her voice made her clasp Willie's arm.

"Yup. It's yellow. And it's not a Land Rover, it's a 1968 Toyota Land Cruiser."

"Sounds cool," Dharma said. "What's it like?"

"Like a Jeep," Dwayne answered. He unwrapped his

own sandwich to reveal two slices of white bread with a fried egg and ketchup in the middle.

Willie pulled a packet of cookies from his pocket and slid them toward Dwayne. "I'm not going to eat these. I'm too focused on the assignment to eat more than this." He bit a bigger bite out of the sandwich. It wasn't the first time he noticed his friend's scant lunch or how hungry he was. Willie had enough to get by but wondered if Dwayne really did. He had been offering his cookies for years. Always with some excuse, because he understood pride and wanted to save his friend from the embarrassment. He wondered if his friend ever got fresh-baked cookies with his mother working all the time. Willie's grandmother always made cookies for the week and provided extra for the church when she had them.

The weekend went by with Willie just barely completing all of his homework before dark on Sunday. He'd taken four hours on the English assignment. "Just double the time she expected. Not bad, Maisy," he said to the dog sitting on the step beside him. He picked up a stick and threw it. Maisy ran into the yard and carried it back, wagging her tail.

Willie decided to walk up the hill to check Baxter's place. It had been months since he and Dwayne tried to muster the courage to go on his property. No one else around would dare go near the place. Everyone knew of old Baxter and his guns. But Willie no longer heard the dogs when Maisy was at his side.

He wandered back down to the house, with the old man's behavior at the forefront of his mind. When he entered the house, his father was sitting at the table with a glass of cold raw milk and exactly two cookies.

"Hey, Dad."

His father looked up at him but didn't speak.

"I've been thinking about the old man next door."

"You mean Baxter?" William Sr. said, plopping a piece of cookie in his mouth. "What about him?"

"Dwayne and I noticed he's not shooting at anyone anymore. I haven't even seen him for a few months now. The dogs aren't barking anymore." Willie added.

"Well, when was the last time you were over there?"

"Summer. We ducked into the barn to avoid getting shot. Stayed there a few hours, but it he never came out."

"Don't suppose you thought to knock on the front door?" his father asked.

"He'd shoot anyone who dared do that."

William Sr. sighed, sipped his milk, and sat back, crossing his leg over his knee. "His water has been running a long time. I'll have the fire department check in on him. Maybe he left. Don't know. He's a quiet, stay-to-himself kind of guy. Serving in Vietnam was no picnic."

"Yeah. I guessed that's why he liked his privacy."

Willie took off up the stairs, hoping his father was right and the man had left.

***

The next day after school, Willie drove home in his Land Cruiser. The excitement of driving the open top vehicle with just a square rollbar was exhilarating. He noticed the firehouse door was open and the truck was gone. There weren't a lot of emergency calls in the winter that he could remember. Although curious, he headed straight toward home, but the road was blocked. He met with the fireman waving for him to drive around.

"Hey, Willie. You headed home?"

"Yeah," Willie said. "What's going on?"

"We were called to do a wellness check and found the resident deceased. Been that way a while," the fireman said.

Willie knew exactly who they were talking about. He didn't hesitate to drive over the rough terrain to get to his house, where he could find out more. Once there, he parked the Land Cruiser, pulled the emergency brake, and left toward the hill and the commotion.

The police were standing outside with the firemen. The crew had cut a large square section of the trailer away for them to access the body. "Willie, thanks to your tip, we were able to find the old man."

"Sad way to go," the chief said.

Willie agreed, but he also believed Baxter went the way he wanted. He didn't believe the man wanted anyone around in his time among the living, so he doubted he'd want someone crowding his side in death. This was a man that cheated death for years in Vietnam; wounded many times. Yet he passed away without any fanfare and alone.

Later in the year, Willie would learn that the old man had been dead for a long time. They had to cut away the section of the trailer because the body was too bloated. The trailer was removed from the lot for investigation, since it was an RV type. The corpses of the dogs lay next to Baxter's body. The sprinkler and lights were on a timer, but the electric company never turned off the power. The coroner concluded he died of a heart attack.

The empty space where the trailer stood still reminded him of the years he and his friend spent dodging the man for their lives, only to discover he had lost his own. Willie pondered nostalgically, remembering the exciting times that were full of adventure, which wouldn't have been the same without the old man.

19

GRADUATION

"Come on, Willie!" Dharma called from the gymnasium doorway. "We're lining up."

Willie was in the hallway, taking in the sight of white cement walls and blue metal lockers. The moment was surreal. *How did time go by so fast?* he thought. The fluorescent lights overhead flickered, a sign a bulb was going to blow. It had been like that for the whole of his senior year. He ran his hand over his locker and the number seventy-eight. The familiar feel of the vents, the lift mechanism, and the smell of someone's gym clothes in a locker next to his, embedded themselves in his memory. *I'm never coming back here. But I'm ready to move forward. I know God has a plan.*

On his way to the gym, he trailed his fingers over the cool painted lines in between the cement blocks. The grout was grainy but oddly smooth from the thick layer of paint. It reminded him of the paint they used on Verga's farm. He used more than his fair share of paint gallons, whitewashing fencing and keeping the old barns from further weathering. The paint was quite different on each surface. *I'll never feel this again.*

Willie peeked into the gym doors where the basketball court was lit only by the emergency light. A place he knew well and had many fun times playing basketball for school pride. He smiled, sighed, and moved on. Though he was good, he wasn't the star. He knew that and accepted it. Playing professional sports was never his goal. Though a few small college offers were in his pocket, he knew it would be a wasted effort. Willie was too practical. Needless to say, he wasn't granted any large school scholarships. No grants or awards would be coming his way because he was not an exceptional student. He was the typical academically average student and accepted that. However, his English teacher had a bit of advice she gave him on the last day of classes.

"Willie," she said. "I wanted to take a moment to share a few thoughts with you. This year has been a journey of growth and learning. You worked hard on literary works that were a personal challenge and your writing skills have greatly improved, showing great promise for a future that will shine bright for anything you choose to do. Who knows, maybe, someday, you'll be a famous lawyer. It has been a pleasure to witness your progress and witness your enthusiasm for the grasping of the subject. I am proud of you. Beyond the academic achievements, I want to commend you for your resilience and adaptability. This year presented numerous challenges. You had work and athletic endeavors while maintaining your job at Verga

Orchards, not to mention your church commitments. Despite these hurdles, you have shown determination, perseverance, and a commitment to your education. Your ability to adapt and thrive in such circumstances is a testament to your strength and dedication. Clearly you were raised right. I commend your parents.

"I hope that this year has not only expanded your knowledge of English but also broadened your perspectives and nurtured your love for learning. Literature has the power to cause us to step back and analyze before jumping into a conclusion with two feet. My hope is that you have found inspiration in the words of great authors and that these stories will continue to resonate with you long after you leave this classroom. After you graduate, I encourage you to keep the spirit of learning alive. Take time to read books that spark your curiosity, write stories that reflect your unique voice, and continue to explore the beauty of language. Use this break to recharge, reflect, and pursue your passions. Take with you the lessons you have learned and all the life skills you have honed.

"I am grateful to have been your teacher and to have witnessed your growth. You have demonstrated resilience, determination, and a commitment to your education. As you move on to new adventures, whether it's college, the workforce, or other paths—like a mission for your church—remember that the skills you have developed and the knowledge you have acquired will serve you well. It has been an honor to be your English teacher. Congratulations, and best of luck in all your endeavors, Willie." She crooked a slight smile, gave him a big hug, and walked away.

Willie was taken by surprise because he hadn't realized the effort he had put forth in his studies was noticed. The students with the highest grades always received all the acknowledgments. Having his teacher's kind and motivational words made him think more about what he planned to do. He loved helping people and felt fulfilled when he was able to do so. Being recognized was one way he knew how to help, but he was also muscular, fit, and physically capable of doing the hard labor people needed when they were no longer able to do it for themselves. Willie was not afraid of work, either. He had the know-how and tenacity to dive into new projects and see them through to the end.

Other paths, he thought. It was as if there were a sign telling him that he was choosing the right course; a way to affect lives. The journey was waiting for him to begin. He had the whole world in front of him and was clearly the type of young man that would push to succeed no matter what he did.

***

Saturday evening arrived.

The graduation ceremony was set to begin at seven in

the evening. The sun was still high in the blue summer sky. Willie's mother and grandmother wore summer dresses while his dad and grandfather dressed in nice overalls. His mother tucked his hair behind his ear, grabbed the black graduation gown that she pressed, and handed it to Willie.

"Your turn. I'm proud of you."

"Thank you, Mom. But high school isn't anything. I'm going to conquer the world." Willie said.

"A lot of boys won't get to graduate this year, with the war and all," his father noted.

"I know, Dad. I have a few classmates who were deployed. They volunteered before the end of senior year, and Dharma's cousin, Jane . . . her brother was killed in action. I'm not sure if they'll make it, but Dharma's immediate family is coming."

"What about Dwayne?" he asked.

"He was called to the draft, but he's the only man of the house. His mom needs him on the farm. They didn't take him," Willie said.

The conversation highlighted the reality that faced all the members of the Collins family, just as it did the rest of the country. The Vietnam War was in full swing, and the draft was pulling young men Willie and Eddie's ages. Mark and Stewart were still too young and had to finish school. Eddie was spared the draft because he was in college. Willie's father had already served two tours in

Korea. Willie knew his father was too old to go back in, though his heart was with the men abroad.

"Well, come on," Cara said. "Enough of this. My boy is graduating, and I want a good seat."

The whole family, including Eddie, piled into the dusty green station wagon. Willie's grandparents followed in their yellow Toyota Hilux pickup truck. Graduation had the entire town talking. The excitement of future dreams and past experiences passed the lips of every customer Willie met at work. The ladies in the farm market even made him a peach pie to celebrate his accomplishment. Willie didn't really see what all the fuss was about but decided to enjoy the attention.

It was a bittersweet moment. After the summer, Willie would no longer be employed at Verga Orchard. His time to move on, though he had no interest in returning to city life. He wanted to remain in the country. He loved farming and the outdoors. The clean, fresh air, the customers, and the beauty that surrounded him night and day could not compare to what Sacramento or any other city offered. He liked not living in a rat race where people lived by the clock. Instead, he lived by the seasons, the weather, and whatever nature dictated. It was unwritten and exciting.

The four boys sat in the backseat; the older boys were over six feet tall. They still smiled and laughed and occasionally hit their heads on the roof of the car or bumped their knees into one another. It reminded Willie of their ride in the car on that first day of their new country life. He was in fifth grade when they moved, but it felt like yesterday. He felt seasoned, yet he also had a sense of renewal. It had been a long time since the six Collins were in the same car, heading to the same venue. Eddie had a car when he was home and when he wasn't Willie used to drive it—that ugly orange 1970 Camaro. They had pickup trucks for local stuff and work. There wasn't really time for family bonding or dinners when all the boys had jobs on farms or in machine shops, or in Willie's case, at the butcher. They were a hardworking, God-fearing, family that put their work ethic to the grind.

William Sr. pulled into a parking space in the middle of the school's parking lot. There were folding chairs set up on the green inside the track. Bleachers were put in place for the guests. He opened the door for Cara while the boys filed out of the car. Willie put his mortarboard on, and Cara straightened the tassel.

"There," she said. "It's on the right side." She kissed his cheek. "You look perfect."

Willie hugged her. "Thank you, Mom."

Willie saw Dharma and jogged off to meet up with her and a few other classmates. He couldn't help the feeling of pride he held inside. He was graduating and about to embark on the next stage of his life. The unknown didn't feel as foreign or surreal. Instead, he felt sure of himself.

Somehow, he knew that his grit and determination would serve him well.

The kids lined up in the gymnasium. They were placed in alphabetical order. Once the familiar *Pomp and Circumstance* started, the loud, excited discussions and laughter that reverberated off the field, silenced. Each young man and woman took their place in line and started the procession to the football field. There were about seventy chairs for the graduates. Willie sidled down the third row and stopped before the chair marked with his name.

When the last student stood before his seat, the band ceased their playing at the end of the phrase with a diminuendo. The principal stepped up to the microphone and the ceremony commenced.

He guided all in attendance through the Pledge of Allegiance while the band played the *Star-Spangled Banner*.

He cleared his throat and gripped the podium. "Graduates, please be seated."

They took their seats. Willie glanced back at Dwayne and Dharma and the other girls he had dated over the last two years. Some had crumpled tissues, blotting their eyes, while others smiled, fully embracing the moment.

"Ladies, gentlemen, faculty, and staff," the principal began, "parents, family, friends, and graduating seniors. Today marks the end of a journey. It is a momentous occasion, for we come together in celebration. But first, let us reflect on the experiences that all who are present overcame, endured, and even thrived. The 1970s are proving to be a time of profound change. We have witnessed cultural, political, and social growth. These experiences have shaped us, challenged us, and ignited a passion within our hearts to strive for a better world. Our students come from a small town, but they have big dreams, strong backs, and minds rooted on a solid foundation to build and reach heights nobody would believe country people could achieve.

"But as you embark on this new phase of your lives, it is essential that you do not forget the lessons you have learned during your time in high school. Your education has equipped you with the knowledge and skills necessary to navigate the complexities of the world. But more than that, your strength is in the community you grew up in, where we help one another. Take that attitude into the world.

"It is also a time to chase your dreams.

"Finally, as you bid farewell to your beloved high school, do not forget to express your gratitude to the teachers, parents, and mentors who have guided you along your journey. Their unwavering support and belief in your potential has been instrumental in your success. Remember to carry their wisdom with you as you embark on new adventures. Always remember where you came from, no matter where you end up. May God bless all of you in your endeavors in life."

Willie realized the truth behind the principal's words. He did, in fact, grow up in a place that was special, where nobody had money, but they did not care. Everyone was poor, so no one knew any better. It was a place of love of country, love of God, love of family, friends, and community. Now Willie wondered how he could convey that to the rest of the world. For that moment, he was lost in deep thought.

The two rows of seniors made their way to the stage, a table with several piles of diplomas waited for their recipients. Willie's row stood. As he neared the green Astroturf platform, he saw the principal slide a diploma from the table and smile. He turned to the microphone and said, "William Collins Jr."

He stepped onto the stage that evening, his hand outstretched to embrace not only the principal's hand but also the symbolic transition. It was time to leave his childhood behind. He ascended the stage as Willie, but he descended as William Collins, a man.

20
WILLIE'S
REFLECTIONS

Willie walked up the hill through the plum trees toward the setting sun. The citrine glow gave way to the deeper blue of the evening. The different shades of pink and yellow drew his attention. He found the spot where he took in the majestic views for the first time, just eight years prior, a transplant from Sacramento. It was a foreign world to him then. A place with no trolley cars, buses, or racing pedestrians. The city kids gathering at the park after school, and the small house with barely a yard, all turned into a distant memory.

The country welcomed him with the first evening sun. And it still welcomed him every moment of every day. The purple and yellow fruits filled the deep green leaves, creating the sense of being home. It was his life, and he was grateful. His devoted companion, Maisy, his grandparents' Irish setter, followed him. Willie took a seat on the stone wall that separated their land from that which had been old man Baxter's.

It was still hard for him to grasp that Baxter was gone. So many of his days were filled with thoughts of escaping the old man's glimpse and eventual crack of the barrel. The days after his passing were left quiet, but Baxter had left his mark. Willie and Dwayne still watched the pasture as they walked along the road where the trailer had been. It was strange not seeing the trailer, but it opened up the view.

Maisy sat at Willie's side. He reached down and scratched the top of her head. The evening quiet was taken over by the now familiar and still welcoming sound of an approaching train. The train reminded him of the simple joys the country offered him. His heart was filled with joy as he cracked a smile and leaned back, sighing.

Thinking back on his youth, he smiled. He knew that he was blessed with a wonderful life. One that was filled with excitement, hard work, hardships, and adventure. Willie laughed when he thought about the first plum fight. He had juice and welts that left him wanting more of the life he now treasured. The Collins Pack was unstoppable. At least until college, a church mission, and family needs pulled them into new roles. Though they vowed to continue their adventures even if it was only once or twice a year.

The last five years, he was working for the big peach and plum farm, embraced good friends, and was God-fearing. Willie sat, realizing that the adventures taught him to work hard. Something that he would carry through life; learning to never give up, work super hard, and love

God and country. The contentment he felt within was because he learned to embrace what he had and build on it—to accept the fortune of life and living.

The peach trees he saved and the land he helped cultivate were vessels for education, but not taught in any classroom or book. He learned the joy behind helping others. When he took the initiative to approach his neighbors and help defeat an outbreak of disease that could have devastated all the farmers in the area, he was filled with a feeling deeper than simple gratification. It marked him in a way that created a desire to help. Through his perseverance, he learned that he did not need to know and understand the whole to bring about change. He had to find the solution and work to bring it forth. And seeing the relief on the face of his neighbors when the disease was eradicated made all the difference. This made him feel that he could accomplish anything in this world.

Even in his puppy love relationships, he learned the impact of his actions. He enjoyed being selfless, wanting to do well by others, and letting them be their own people. All the girls he knew, and the ones he didn't, had long hair and a natural beauty. They were good people filled with kindness. Dharma and all the other girls in the school welcomed him. He learned to listen and how to embrace relationships with an open mind and heart.

Yes, he thought about all the good, but thought about

the struggle at times, too. Getting into fights, trying to find his place in the community—relishing in relinquishing the bullies and always sticking up for the small guy.

The train drew closer, and Willie hugged the Irish setter. "I don't know that there's anything better than this, Maisy. My life has been good." After the train passed, he pushed away from the stone wall and walked to the crest of the hill. The creaking cars and familiar squeal of metal wheels on the metal rails held a rhythm that he learned over the years. It brought life to the country. The approach rumbled; the departure wailed. A haunting reminder of a bustling life somewhere beyond. Maybe Sacramento, maybe Lake Tahoe. Though to Willie, it didn't matter. The train itself was a part of the masterpiece. It's precipice—the high-pitched warning before disappearing in the tunnel.

Below Willie and Maisy, the valley stretched for miles. The distant hills were purple mounds under the now darkened sky. The navy blue of night was dappled with white stars. It made him wonder what lay ahead. His future was unwritten. But there was one thing he knew for certain. He was ready to conquer the world, no matter what he decided. Though before that, he wanted to serve God and go on a mission to serve others.

It was the last night of his childhood. But he took refuge in knowing that many more lay ahead where the soothing sound of creaking cars and rumbling tracks would continue to capture his heart, enveloping him in the music of the valley and the majesty of the rolling country hills. It was the lullaby of trains, and a sign of a life well lived.

EPILOGUE

As Willie embarked on his new journey, he learned to transition into a different world where one had to survive on their own. He chose to serve a mission for his church to help fellow citizens and those who were downtrodden. In this time, he grew physically, mentally, spiritually, and academically. Willie went off to college and tackled the All-American dream of wife, child, and career all by the age of twenty-two.

What would the future bring? It was unknown. But what Willie knew for sure was that he loved growing up in the country and loved the community. And someday, he would figure out how to convey that to others. Because as Willie learned; there are no problems, only challenges. And he liked finding solutions.

ABOUT
FREDERICK W. PENNEY

Fred Penney, Injury Lawyer® has the highest AVVO personal injury attorney rating of a 10– "Superb Lawyer". Frederick W. Penney is an AV Preeminent rated Attorney by Martindale Hubbell, one of the most prestigious ratings systems in the United States. This is the highest possible rating in both legal ability and ethical standards. Mr. Penney has also been rated AV Preeminent by the opinions of the members of the Judiciary. Frederick Penney has been appointed by the Placer County Court as a Settlement Conference Judge, better known as a Judge Pro-Tem. Mr. Penney preforms this duty only on occasion. For over 30 years Mr. Penney and his firm have handled many high profile and substantial injury cases including product liability, trucking accidents, escalator and elevator accidents, helicopter and plane accidents, boating accidents among others.

Mr. Penney is the host of *Radio Law Talk*, a radio

show discussing the latest trending legal topics and news. Radio Law Talk is broadcast throughout many areas and can be found on SRN Radio networks.

Frederick Penney as "has been featured in *Forbes, USA Today, Super Lawyers Magazine* among many other prestigious publications

ACCOLADES

- *Attorney at Law* magazine's 2023 Attorney of the Year
- Lifetime Achievement Award America's Top 100 Attorneys
- Member Million Dollar Advocate Forum
- Member Multi-million Dollar Advocate Forum
- Sacramento Magazines Top Lawyers 2015-to present
- AVVO 10.0 Superb Rating for Personal Injury
- AVVO Client's Choice for Personal Injury
- AV Preeminent by Attorney Peers and by the Judiciary
- AV Preeminent
- RUE Ratings Best Attorneys of America Lifetime Rating
- Super Lawyers Rated Attorney
- Super Lawyer Northern California 2019
- www.penneylawyers.com/
- radiolawtalk.com/